THE DICK FRANCIS COMPANION

Jean Swanson &
Dean James

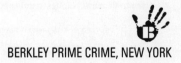

BERKLEY PRIME CRIME, NEW YORK

THE DICK FRANCIS COMPANION

A Berkley Prime Crime Book / published by arrangement with
Jean Swanson and Dean James

PRINTING HISTORY
Berkley Prime Crime trade paperback edition / August 2003

Library of Congress Cataloging-in-Publication Data

Swanson, Jean (Jean R.)
The Dick Francis companion / Jean Swanson & Dean James.
p. cm.
ISBN 0-425-18187-1 (alk. paper)
1. Francis, Dick—Criticism and interpretation—Handbooks, manuals, etc. 2. Detective and mystery stories, English—Handbooks, manuals, etc. 3. Horse racing in literature—Handbooks, manuals, etc. 4. Crime in literature—Handbooks, manuals, etc. I. James, Dean (Darryl Dean) II. Title.

PR6056.R27Z68 2003
823'.914—dc21
2003051954

For my brother,
Eric Arthur Swanson,
childhood coconspirator in all things bookish,
who has a lifelong devotion to the printed word.
(JS)

For Edith Brown,
the best "big sister"
a guy could have.
Aren't you glad I talked
you into reading Dick Francis?
(DJ)

ACKNOWLEDGMENTS

From Jean: Thanks go, as always, to Dean: longtime friend and invaluable coauthor. Nobody ever believes it when I tell them that Dean and I have never had a single argument while writing books together—but it's true! Who could argue with Dean's cheerfulness and impeccable Southern manners? I'd like to thank our agent, Nancy Yost, and our editor at Berkley, Natalee Rosenstein, for their support, good advice, and help over the years. I would like also to thank my colleague and fellow Dick Francis fan Sandi Richey for her extraordinary help in finding materials. Everyone at the University of Redlands knows Sandi's reputation for helping people. Tam McPhail at the Stromness Books and Prints shop in Orkney went to a good deal of trouble to find an essential book; many thanks to him. And, as ever, I thank my husband Jim Thompson for his unfailing support, patience, and creative help, and for everything that matters most.

From Dean: first, a special thanks to my coauthor, Jean Swanson, for her years of friendship and for making working on books together a joy rather than a job. Second, thanks to our agent, Nancy Yost, and to our editor, Natalee Rosenstein, for always making the work as painless as possible. What a great support team! Third, thanks to the dear friends who make daily life supportable: Megan Bladen-Blinkoff, Elizabeth Foxwell, Martha Farrington, Julie Herman, Angela Miller, and David Thompson. Finally, a special thanks to Francis fan and collector, Charles Bell, who introduced me to the (sadly, short-lived) magazine on Texas horse racing published by Leif Glensgaard and Bill Freeman, of National Publishing Inc., in Houston. I very much appreciate the information gleaned from their publication.

And special thanks to Felix and Dick Francis for their invaluable assistance in the preparation of this book.

CONTENTS

INTRODUCTION

Welcome to the world of Dick Francis.

Be prepared for malice lurking behind an innocuous facade.

Be prepared for danger in the most ordinary of activities.

Be prepared to hang on for dear life.

Such is the world of Dick Francis, one of the world's best-selling and beloved writers of high-octane suspense fiction. For nearly four decades Dick Francis penned a book a year, compiling an impressive body of work, achieving a popularity and a longevity that few, if any, of his peers in the world of crime writing can match.

Many think of Dick Francis as that guy who writes about horses. To a certain extent, this is true. Many of Francis's novels are somehow connected to the world of horse racing, chiefly steeplechase racing. But Francis wisely realized, early on in his thriller-writing career, that he shouldn't always depend on the world of English racing for the background of each and every book. While many of his heroes over the years have some connection to racing, Francis has given us books with wonderfully diverse backgrounds: banking, winemaking, glassblowing, flying, filmmaking, gemstones . . . just to name a few. Francis has the knack of making each of these worlds interesting and accessible to readers, providing a fascinating frame on which to hang his tales of mayhem and murder.

The heroes in Francis novels are as varied, in many respects, as the backgrounds of the books. Characters like Sid Halley, Kit Fielding, Thomas Lyon, and Rob Finn have some characteristics in common, but each also has something about him that makes him distinctive from the rest. Kit Fielding, for example, has an almost psychic ability to communicate with the horses he rides, while Thomas Lyon has the gift of visual imagination, which makes a director into a filmmaker of extraordinary vision. What all these heroes share, however, is a fundamental decency that compels them, when the chips are down, to fight to their very last breath to defeat villainy in its many forms.

Perhaps it is this quality above all others, the capacity of an ordinary man to become a hero under the right circumstances, that has made Dick Francis so hugely popular around the world, crossing many linguistic and cultural boundaries. Readers, male and female alike, can identify with a Francis hero as he fights, despite sometimes overwhelming odds, for something he believes in, something worth dying for, if necessary. Readers can take great comfort, though, in knowing that a Francis hero will not only persevere, he will triumph. The good guy wins, having been tested to his utmost along the way.

This book is intended, first, as a tribute to the writer who has entertained millions of readers for the last forty years and become an annual fixture on international best-seller lists. Second, it is a reader's guide designed to help readers search out particular information about their favorite Francis novels. For example, in which Francis novel was the hero a toy maker? Which books are about Sid Halley? Third, for the reader just discovering the joys of a Francis novel, it will serve as an introduction to a fascinating body of work.

We invite you to join us in revisiting, if you're longtime fans like us, or in discovering, if you're relatively new to his work, the world of Dick Francis.

Jean Swanson and Dean James

BIOGRAPHICAL INFORMATION

Richard Stanley Francis was born in 1920 on his grandparents' farm, Coedcanlas, in South Wales. His father managed a stable of hunters at Holyport near Maidenhead, but Dick and his older brother Douglas spent many happy summers and holidays at Coedcanlas, and Dick learned to ride there. He soon graduated to racing and show jumping: "The first race I ever won was an apple-bobbing contest at a gymkhana when I was eight." He always wanted to be a jockey, but when he left school, he went to work with his father, riding and training hunters. During World War II he served in the Royal Air Force (1940–1946). The RAF decided to train him as an aircraft mechanic, but he was not satisfied with his lot and constantly bombarded the RAF with requests to train as a pilot. Francis spent two years in the North African desert: "We patched and mended the torn bodies of the planes as they landed, getting them back into the air again as soon as we could." Eventually his request to fly was granted, and he trained as a fighter pilot in Africa. He was transferred back to England in 1944, and flew fighters and bombers, including Spitfires and Lancasters.

After the war ended, Dick met Mary Brenchley at his cousin's wedding and fell in love at first sight. They were married in 1947. Mary contracted polio while pregnant with their first child, and was hospitalized in an iron lung. She fought hard against the effects of the illness, and their son Merrick was born in 1950. A second son, Felix, was born in 1953.

Following his wartime service, Francis worked briefly with his father, then first entered the world of racing in 1946 as an amateur jockey. He turned professional in March 1948, and became a famous jockey in National Hunt racing. He won more than 350 races, was Champion Jockey in 1953–54, and was retained as a jockey to Queen Elizabeth, the Queen Mother, from 1953 until January 1957. Francis rode eight times in the famous Grand National Steeplechase, and nearly won in 1956 when his horse, the Queen Mother's Devon Loch, suddenly collapsed only forty yards from victory. It was, he says, "both the high point and low point of my career as a jockey." To this day, nobody knows for certain why Devon Loch collapsed; it's still a mystery.

In 1957, Francis suffered another serious fall and decided to retire while he was still at the top of his career. He published his autobiography, *The Sport of Queens*, later that year. "I was lucky to have my first efforts published, as most writers fill copious wastebaskets before this happens, and I know that if this first book had been rejected everywhere I would never have written another." He was also invited to write racing articles for the *London Sunday Express*, and wrote for them for sixteen years.

Dick Francis turned to writing novels when, as he says, "the threadbare state of a carpet and a rattle in my car" caused him to realize that he needed to make more money. His first novel, *Dead Cert*, was published in 1962. He and Mary traveled and did extensive research for the succeeding novels. Mary learned to fly small planes as part of their research for *Flying Finish*, and she enjoyed it so much that she went on to earn her instrument rating, and eventually to write a textbook for pilots of small planes. Dick and Mary traveled by bus all over the

United States for *Blood Sport*, and traveled to many locations around the world for later novels.

Since 1954, the Francis family had lived in the village of Blewbury, "where the Berkshire Downs sweep gently towards the Thames Valley." In 1980, Dick and Mary moved to Florida; in 1992, they moved to the Caribbean island of Grand Cayman (where part of *Second Wind* is set). Mary Francis died in the Cayman Islands in September 2000.

Dick Francis's thirty-eighth best-selling novel, *Shattered*, was published in the United States by Putnam in 2000. In addition to his novels and autobiography, Francis has also published a biography of the famous British jockey Lester Piggott, *A Jockey's Life*, and a collection of short stories, *Field of Thirteen*. His novels have been translated into more than thirty languages, and he has received acclaim from critics and readers all over the world. Dick Francis has received three Edgar Allan Poe Awards for Best Novel (for *Forfeit*, *Whip Hand*, and *Come to Grief*), and the Mystery Writers of America named him a Grand Master in 1996. The British Crime Writers Association awarded him a Silver Dagger Award for *For Kicks*, a Gold Dagger Award for *Whip Hand*, and the Cartier Diamond Dagger for his works in 1990. Tufts University awarded him an honorary doctorate of humane letters in 1991. Dick Francis was elected to be a fellow of the Royal Society of Literature in 1998, and, in America, the Malice Domestic convention gave him their Lifetime Achievement Award in 2000. Dick Francis was made an officer of the Order of the British Empire (OBE) in 1984, and named a commander of the Order of the British Empire (CBE) in the Queen's Birthday Honours List of 2000.

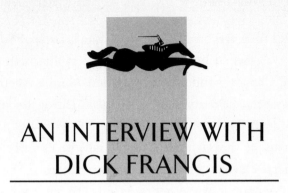

AN INTERVIEW WITH DICK FRANCIS

Q: Before you started writing the thrillers, you worked in two very demanding professions, racing and journalism, in which self-discipline is of great importance. What experiences would you say gave you the best training for your later writing career?

I wrote hundreds of letters home during my six years in the Royal Air Force during the Second World War. For much of the time I was stationed in Africa so my letters had to be short and to the point and also I tried to convey to my family details of how things were progressing without falling foul of the censor who, understandably, didn't want us to say anything about where we were or what we were doing. This was good training for my years as a journalist. I learned very quickly that in the world of newspapers the first call on space is for the advertisements. I was never able to get a superfluous word past my editor. This taught me to be lean and tight in my writing and this was such good training for writing novels.

Q: Did you ever think about becoming a trainer after retiring as a jockey? Would you have turned to writing, do you think, if you had done so?

In 1956 I rode Devon Loch in the Grand National Steeplechase. The horse was owned by Her Majesty Queen Elizabeth the Queen Mother and I had a wonderful ride around Aintree racetrack where the race has been held annually since 1839. Devon Loch and I had jumped 30 great fences and raced more than four and a half miles when, with just 40 yards left to the finish and with us well clear in front of the others, Devon Loch collapsed beneath me. The horse did recover and went on to win other races but at the time it was a disaster of massive proportions. I was approached to write my autobiography by a shrewd literary agent who saw a financial opportunity for us both. I had written half of this when I decided to retire from race riding after a bad fall. The then editor of the *London Sunday Express* reckoned that if I had half written a book I might be able to put a few words together so he invited me to write half a dozen articles for his newspaper. Those half a dozen articles went on for 16 years full employment. So I didn't have time to think about being a trainer, which I didn't want to be anyway.

Q: Critics and historians of the genre have sometimes said that your heroes are an Everyman-type figure and therefore very similar to one another. Do you think this is a fair assessment? If not, why not? Have you enjoyed creating main characters who aren't jockeys or jockeys who have gone on to other professions? Did that help keep the writing fresh and challenging for you?

All my protagonists react to situations as I would react in the same circumstances so, yes I suppose it is a fair assessment to claim that they are similar in many ways. My heroes may all be humble and self-reliant, but above all they possess courage and a sense of right and wrong. They are able to withstand great pressure both from mental torment and physical pain, and they are strong, decent and chivalrous; but they are "ordinary" men, not super-human James Bond types. They employ their multi-talented resourcefulness to solve a mystery without the need to demonstrate insight beyond the capability of man. Their differences are reflected in their choices of career and changes in taste—minor but significant. Even though my heroes may be similar, I have not generally written a long series of novels around a single character. Sid Halley appears three times in novels written over thirty years, and Kit Fielding occurs just twice. All the others are "one offs." I find it helps to fill the pages if the main character has a varied background. If all the main characters were jockeys or ex jockeys I think that the stories would be very limited. My publishers always wanted me to keep the stories in the world of horseracing but, at times, the links have been somewhat tenuous.

Q: *How do you find names for your characters? How about the names for the horses? Have any of your readers ever used the names of horses in your work to name their own?*

I think that the best source of names for characters and horses are place names. I use names I see on road signs in England. Many of my lead characters have been named in this way. Daniel Roke appears in *For Kicks* and Roke is the name of a small village near to where I used to live. Alan York in *Dead Cert*, Edward Lincoln in *Smokescreen* and David Cleveland in *Slay-Ride* are just a few other examples. I am aware that people have indeed used my horse names to name real horses but, when I wrote a book, I did make sure that no registered racehorse in England had a name I chose to use in it.

Q: *How important is the beginning of each book?*

I like to catch my readers on the very first page, preferably with the first line. Grab the reader in the first paragraph and never let go. How about "Art Mathews shot himself loudly and messily in the centre of the parade ring at Dunstable races" or "Kerry Sanders looked like no angel of death" or "The Earl of October drove into my life in a light blue Holden that had seen better days, and death and destruction tagged along for the ride." Try putting them back on the shelf, and that is only three of thirty-eight novels.

Q: Only a few times have you repeated heroes, with Sid Halley appearing three times over the years and Kit Fielding appearing twice, back to back. Did you ever think about writing a long series, like many mystery writers do? Why did you bring back Sid Halley in Whip Hand *and* Come to Grief? *(Both of which won Edgar Awards for Best Novel.)*

Sid Halley (Halley rhymes with valley) first appeared in 1965 in *Odds Against*. In 1979 a British television company made a series of six programs using my novel *Odds Against* and five new stories. Sid Halley was played by a Welsh actor called Mike Gwilym. The programs were very successful but sadly they did not make any more. My wife, Mary, and I became good friends with Mike and we asked him to come and stay with us one weekend during a break in the filming. As he sat down in our sitting room on the first evening I asked him what he would like to drink. "Scotch." As I handed the drink to him it was just as if I was handing it to Sid Halley. I immediately thought that I must write another story using Sid. At the end of *Odds Against* Sid loses his hand and so a new door was opened to research on prosthetic limbs. Mary and I went to the Artificial Limb Centre at Roehampton Hospital in England to see the latest myoelectric hands that were available. These limbs were incorporated into my new novel, *Whip Hand*, and also into the TV series. Sid returned again in *Come to Grief* as a result of continuous pressure from my readers to have him back. Although the three novels were written with fourteen years between the first two and a further sixteen years to the last one, Sid is timeless with only a few months passing in "Sid-time" between the stories.

I believe very strongly that a good story demands that the characters within it develop both in their attitudes and also in their relationships with the other characters. It is this development which attracts the reader to continue to read to discover where each person is going to end up. Without a road of discovery of each character the story is wooden and uninteresting. I would, consequently, find it difficult to write a whole series around a single character without the order in which they are read becoming all-important and possibly confusing.

Relationships between my protagonist and female characters in my novels are important to me. In *Forfeit* it was the relationship between a man and his invalid wife that was paramount, and how the existence of an affair changes that relationship: guilt / understanding—desire / love. In *Bonecrack* I greatly enjoyed creating the interaction between sons and fathers and the relationship between the sons and how this impacted on the father / son situation. Writing is very hard work but it is also fun to make the characters dance to one's own tune.

Q: With Kit Fielding, you wrote two books in a row about the same main character. When you were writing Break In, *did you know you'd be writing another book so soon about Kit?*

Immediately after finishing *Break In* I had to write the biography of Lester Piggott, one of England's greatest jockeys, which was published in America as *A Jockey's Life*. I finished that just as I was due to start the next novel. I had no time to research new characters so I used Kit Fielding, Daniel, Princess Casilia and the other characters from *Break In* in *Bolt*.

Q: You've been quoted as saying that you have lived in two worlds: racing and writing. Do you think that this helps account for the success of your books? Do you think American readers like your books because the British racing world seems exotic to them?

I like to think that my books have been successful not just because they are English, or set in an apparently "exotic" world, but because they are well written and because I tell a good story. I receive many thousands of letters from readers, many of them American, who tell me that they re-read them over and over again and that they never become tired of them. I am pleased by that.

Q: You've always been very open about giving your late wife Mary credit for her assistance in the writing of the books. What kinds of advice or input did she give? For example, did she give you insights for the women characters?

Mary and I worked as a team. We discussed everything and she was a master at research with a terrific memory for detail. I have often said that I would have been happy to have both our names on the cover. Mary's family always called me Richard due to having another Dick in the family. I am Richard, Mary was Mary, and Dick Francis was the two of us together.

Q: Which parts of the writing process did you find the easiest? And which were the hardest? For example, many writers complain that the middle part of the book is the most difficult.

I cannot start to write until I have main plot and main character in my mind and this dictates the area of research. Sometimes the character brings both the plot and the place. Other times the idea for the "dirty deed" came early and thus dictates the scene in which the characters are set. For some novels the "scene" has been the primary starting point and research into a situation will throw up a possible motive for skulduggery. The very beginning takes a long time to get it right. After that the story flows quite well for a while but I always find the end the most difficult part. I am usually short of time as the deadline approaches. I do find writing hard work and the continuous need to never miss a day and get five hundred words down on paper before tea becomes very draining.

Q: In other interviews, you've been quoted as saying that basically you write one draft of a book, and that's it. Are there any exceptions to this? Do you do revisions at any stage of the process?

I used to discuss each day's work with Mary and if revisions were needed they were made then rather than rewriting the whole novel at the end. My first finished attempt is therefore the final version. I have a bit of a reputation amongst publishers for refusing to make changes to my finished work. I fight with editors.

Q: Do you have any particular words of advice for a writer who aspires to write thrillers? What do you consider the most important ingredients for a successful thriller?

Know your subject. Research thoroughly and keep the plot boiling. Surprise your readers.

Q: You've been writing novels for forty years now, producing them steadily year after year. Did you ever feel like the pace was too much, that you needed more time to relax between books? How much time did you get to take off between books?

For more than 35 years my routine varied very little. I would start writing in January and the deadline for the manuscript to get to the publishers was mid May. Proof copies would arrive in three to four weeks and I would have to read them over and over to correct the printing errors. I would then take a summer rest and a holiday. All the time I would keep my eyes and ears open to think of a new story and to do some early research. Publication was in September or October and I would spend a few weeks doing some promotion work in both the UK and the USA and sometimes in Canada or Australia and New Zealand. Then there would be a month or two of serious thought and research ready to begin writing again in January. I became used to the routine and I enjoyed it. I retired from the merry-go-round in 2000 when my darling Mary passed away. Since then I have written a few newspaper articles and I have been slowly working on a tribute to Mary.

Q: You've lived in various places while you've been writing: Berkshire (where many scenes in the books are set), Florida, and now the Caymans. Were any of these places easier to write in? How important do you feel a sense of place is to your books? Did you always visit the settings for each book for research?

I discovered that as long as I have a pencil and a notebook I can write anywhere. I moved to Florida from England in 1986 and then to the Cayman Islands in 1992. I have enjoyed writing in all those places, especially in Cayman where I can see the white sand and the deep blue Caribbean Sea from my desk. Almost all of my books have been set in England and my main character has always been British. I know what a British character would think and it is vital to get things right. I almost always visited the scene where the book was set. *For Kicks* starts in Australia and a friend was able to describe the scene for me as I did not go there until ten years later when researching *In the Frame*. However, I went to Norway for *Slay-Ride*, Moscow for *Trial Run*, South Africa for *Smokescreen*, America for *Blood Sport*, and Canada for *The Edge*. Parts of *Second Wind* are set in the Cayman Islands so that research was easy.

Q: Do you have a favourite among your books?

I always used to say that the latest book was my favourite as it was so fresh in my mind and the lead character was so well known to me. Now that I have not written a novel for two years I am able to look back at all the books with an equal affection. I suppose that *Forfeit* will always be a favourite. James Tyrone, the protagonist, is a Sunday newspaperman as I was when I wrote it. His wife suffered from the after affects of polio and so did my wife (although not as badly as Eliz-

abeth in the novel). It was the first of my novels to win an Edgar Allen
Poe Award from the Mystery Writers of America for best novel and
also the Gold Dagger from the Crime Writers Association in England.
But all my books are like my children, I love them equally.

*Q: Do you still keep up with the racing world? Which of the racecourses
is your favourite?*

I try to keep up with the racing world in England. I have the *London Times* delivered to my home each day but it arrives in the Cayman
Islands a day late. Not much good for betting but I never did much of
that anyway. As I get older I find I know fewer and fewer of the racing
characters who seem to get younger and younger. I do go racing
whenever I can and in the last year I have been to the Kentucky Derby,
to the Melbourne Cup in Australia and to race meets in Hong Kong
and all over England. My favourite racecourse has to be Aintree in
spite of it being the scene of my greatest disaster with Devon Loch in
1956. I am a trustee of the fund that was raised by public subscription
to buy the course and save the race in 1983 when there was a move to
close the course and build homes on the land. I return to England each
spring for the running of the Grand National Steeplechase. I also love
the small country racecourse at Bangor-on-Dee in North Wales. It is
such a friendly place with many old friends always present. I rode my
first winner there in 1947 and it remains one of my favourite places. I
also rode many winners, including two Welsh Grand Nationals, at
another favourite track at Chepstow in South Wales.

*Q: You've won many awards, in both careers. Are there any you would
cite as particularly meaningful? Do you think the writing awards helped boost
your career?*

My two most prized racing awards are a silver platter for becoming
the champion jockey in England in 1954 and a solid silver cigarette box

which the Queen Mother gave to me after the Grand National in 1956. My writing career has brought more with four Edgar Allen Poe Awards together with Silver, Gold and Diamond Dagger Awards. But the most pleasing was when I was elected to become a Fellow of the Royal Society of Literature in London. I was delighted when I was granted an honorary doctorate in 1991 by Tufts University in Boston and also when the Queen created me a Commander of the most excellent order of the British Empire for service to literature in 2000. All these awards have provided an important boost to my career and they remain a great joy to me.

Q: In other interviews over the years, you have mentioned your regrets over not winning the Grand National. Are there any other regrets in your long and distinguished career?

Other than not winning that race, I have no real regrets. I have now stopped serious writing although I have done a few articles and some short pieces for charity publications. I have had four different adult careers: wartime RAF pilot, professional steeplechase jockey, newspaperman and author. I have retired four times now and I think that will be it. My darling wife, Mary, died in September 2000 after 53 years of married bliss. I don't suppose I will be that long in following her. Do they take on astronauts at 81?

Q: Finally, is there any special message you'd like to send to your many readers around the world, both old and new, who might be reading this book?

Thank You. Thank you for reading my books, thank you for buying them, and thank you for all the kind letters and cards I have received from so many wonderful people all over the world. I hope you will go on enjoying my books for many years to come but sadly there will be no new ones.

© Dick Francis

August 1, 2002

"TELL ME A STORY, AND TELL IT STRONG AND QUICK": THE NOVELS OF DICK FRANCIS

With the publication of *Shattered* (Putnam, 2000), Dick Francis has published thirty-eight novels and one short-story collection. We have summarized the plot of each novel and the short story collection in this chapter. For more information, you'll simply have to read (or reread) the books!

Dead Cert (1962)

Amateur jockey Major Bill Davidson dies after his horse, Admiral, suffers a fall on the racecourse. His good friend, another amateur jockey, Alan York, witnesses the fall and realizes something was slightly odd about it. After the race, he investigates and discovers that there had been a wire stretched across part of the course. The horse was deliberately felled. But by the time Alan can get someone to check what he's found, the wire has disappeared. Alan continues to delve into the murder of his friend, wondering whether the accident was staged to prevent Admiral from winning the race or to kill Bill Davidson. He soon runs afoul of a gang involved in an extortion racket, and a similar attempt is made on his own life during a race. But Alan perseveres in tracking the threat to its source, uncovering a racket to fix races, and in an exciting, extended chase scene, he eludes his pursuers on the gallant Admiral by riding cross country.

Nerve (1964)

The son of famous classical musicians, Rob Finn has struck out on his own and is just starting a career as a National Hunt steeplechase jockey. His parents understand nothing of his life and his devotion to racing. Although disapproving and remote figures, they are kind to him.

After a fellow jockey is badly injured, Rob gets a chance to substitute for him, and he succeeds brilliantly. Rob brings in winner after winner for several weeks until, mysteriously, his mounts start performing poorly. Everyone blames Rob, and the rumors start going around that he has lost his nerve. He loses his job, and trainers and owners don't want him to ride their horses. Several other jockeys have been accused recently of unreliability and of losing their nerve, and they too have lost their rides and their reputations. But when it happens to him, Rob fights back. In a climactic scene, the villain hangs Rob from a hook in an abandoned stable, throws buckets of cold water over him, and leaves him to die or at least be severely crippled. Afterward, Rob concocts a scheme to destroy the villain in a way similar to what he's suffered. He ruins his reputation, causes him to lose his job, and to feel great mental and emotional pain. It's a highly satisfactory plot device, since it can appeal to any readers who have ever wanted to take revenge on someone who has done them wrong. The novel is spare, taut, and exciting, and Rob is firmly in the tradition of young, bright, principled Dick Francis heroes.

For Kicks (1965)

The stewards of the National Hunt Committee seek the assistance of Daniel Roke, English-born owner of a successful stud farm in Australia, to uncover the facts in what they suspect is a new method of doping racehorses to ensure that they will win races. All attempts to uncover the nature of the drug being used have been fruitless, and the stewards decide that perhaps an operative working undercover will be able to succeed where previous efforts have failed. A journalist had been investigating, but he was killed in a car accident, and the stewards suspect foul play. Daniel Roke transforms himself into a seedy-looking character with an eye to the main chance in order to get close to the principals in the scheme. By diligent investigating and backbreaking hard work in various stables, Daniel eventually figures out the nature of the scheme that turns ordinary racers into winning steeplechasers. The details of the scheme are horribly repugnant, of a nature so vicious that Daniel is more than ever determined to see it stopped. Despite a nearly successful attempt on his life, he is able to defeat the villains and in the process save the life of one of the young women he has met in the course of the investigation. Upon the conclusion of the investigation, he realizes that he will not be happy to go back to his life in Australia, and with the aid of one of the stewards of the National Hunt Committee, he is able to start a new career.

Odds Against (1965)

Dick Francis doesn't often write novels with a series character, but he has written three books featuring investigator and former steeplechase jockey Sid Halley. *Odds Against* is the first in this series, and like many Francis novels it's about courage, especially courage under adversity. Sid, a champion jockey, had to retire from racing after a serious fall that badly injured one of his hands. The damaged hand is wasted and ugly now, and Sid tries to hide his disability from everyone. He has been given a job of sorts with the Hunt Radnor private eye agency, but he takes little interest in his work or in much of anything. The novel begins with Sid underestimating Thomas Andrews, a petty crook who unexpectedly shoots him in the gut one night. As he is recovering, his father-in-law, Admiral Charles Roland, decides that Sid needs a strong jolt to make him interested in life again. Thus he sets him up to be cruelly underestimated and humiliated by Howard Kraye, a crooked speculator whom Charles suspects of trying to destroy Seabury racecourse so he can sell the land for housing developments. Sid meets Charles's challenge, and Kraye doesn't suspect that a broken-down jockey from a poverty-stricken background could be smart enough and persistent enough to uncover his villainous schemes. But Sid, with the help of sidekick Chico Barnes, finally takes to detecting like a duck to water.

In the course of his investigation, Sid meets Zanna Martin, whose face has been badly damaged in a fireworks accident, and he learns from her how to deal with the stares and rudeness of others who see him only in terms of his disability. Miss Martin takes a risk in providing him with some essential information, and he is able to uncover how the complicated racecourse fraud has been set up. The villains eventually come after him, though, and in a memorable scene, Sid is chased through the empty racecourse at night, then tied to a boiler that has been set to blow up. His damaged hand is injured even further, but he finds enough courage even to handle the threat of losing it completely. At the end he suffers grievously, but he has regained his self-respect and some self-confidence, and has embarked upon a rewarding and exciting new career as a racing detective.

This novel was made into a television movie, and Francis thought actor Mike Gwilym did such a good job at depicting Sid Halley that he wrote *Whip Hand*, the second Halley novel, and dedicated it to Gwilym.

Flying Finish (1966)

Henry Grey is an amateur jockey who also flies small planes on the weekends, and has a dull job at an air freight firm in London. He is properly Lord Henry Grey, but he downplays his noble background; it's other people who won't let him forget about it and who make assumptions about what a lord should and shouldn't do with his life. Henry dislikes the aristocratic lifestyle, and he just wants to earn enough money to keep flying and riding, which are the real loves of his life. Shortly after the novel opens, he changes jobs to work for another transport firm, Yardman. There he deals mostly with the air transport of horses, and goes with the horses on the trips. People think that he's just a glorified stable lad, and his family are horrified that he won't get a better job, marry an aristocratic girl who has plenty of money, and come back to the family mansion to live. But Henry's new job combines flying and horses, so he is fairly content, at least until events overcome him and he is dragged into a whirlwind of violence, love, and hate. On a trip to Milan, he meets Gabriella Barzini, who works at the airport gift shop, and they fall in love at first sight. Meanwhile, Henry discovers that one of his colleagues at the transport firm is working a complex fiddle on the company. And, most ominously, men who he works with keep disappearing, generally on flights to Italy. Billy Watkins, one of the other horse handlers, despises Henry for his aristocratic background, and keeps picking vicious fights with him on the flights. Billy's violence reaches a crescendo on a flight to Italy when they are carrying a mysterious passenger as well as a cargo of horses. There is a superb concluding scene (a "flying finish") in which the seriously injured Henry, who has only ever flown small planes, must

escape from his attackers and pilot a large cargo plane safely back to
England from Italy.

Blood Sport (1967)

English intelligence agent Gene Hawkins is set to begin three weeks of
much-needed leave from his job when his boss, Simon Keeble, calls
with a seemingly innocuous invitation to a boating outing. Battling a
severe depression, induced by his job and by his unhappiness over an
unrequited love affair, Gene accedes to his boss's request. He meets
the boss's daughter, beautiful young Lynnie, as well as an old friend of
Keeble's, American millionaire, Dave Teller. Teller has a one-eighth
share in the stallion Chrysalis, which has recently disappeared.
Chrysalis is the third stallion of international status to have disappeared in the last decade. Keeble and Teller work on Gene, trying to
get him to tackle the case of the missing horses, telling him that his
background makes him a natural choice for the job. Gene had grown
up in a training stable in Yorkshire, and he has the necessary knowledge of horses and the racing world to give him an edge. During the
boating outing, an accident lands Dave Teller in hospital. A photo-
graph taken by Keeble's young son, Peter, helps Gene figure out that it
was no accident but a deliberate attempt on Dave Teller's life. Shortly
afterward, Gene leaves for the United States. He goes first to the
offices of the Buttress Life Insurance company, issuers of the policy on
the missing stallion, Chrysalis, where he meets investigator Walt
Prensela. At first suspicious of Gene's ability to succeed where he has
so far failed, Walt soon becomes a friend to Gene. He recognizes
Gene's depression for what it is and does his best to steer Gene away
from suicidal behavior. Ultimately, Walt is the one person who is able
to snap Gene out of his depression, but at considerable cost to himself
and his family. Gene follows the trail of the missing horses across the

United States, with stops in Kentucky and California. He meets Dave Teller's bored, alcoholic wife, Eunice, who tries to tempt him into betraying Dave's confidence, but Gene offers her a different solution to her boredom. The investigation leads Gene to a guest ranch in Wyoming, where he makes an important discovery and identifies the likely suspects in the case. The trail leads him further, to California, and the horse farm of a man who will be Dave Teller's neighbor, once Dave and his wife complete their move from Kentucky. Gene then orchestrates a clever campaign to return Chrysalis to his rightful owners and see that the horse thieves are brought to justice.

Forfeit (1969)

James "Ty" Tyrone is a journalist whose specialty is racing. He works for the none-too-respectable paper, the *Sunday Blaze*, and takes free-lance assignments whenever possible. His wife, Elizabeth, is confined to an iron lung, thanks to a bout with poliomyelitis, and caring for her physically is a tremendous drain on the finances. When the features editor of the magazine *Tally* offers Ty a chance to do a glossy article on the upcoming Lamplighter Gold Cup, Ty is therefore eager to earn some extra money, little dreaming that the assignment will draw him into a very dangerous situation. Ty encounters an older journalist of his acquaintance, Bert Checkov, whose dependence on alcohol has made him a byword among his peers. Deep in his cups, Checkov adjures Ty never to sell his column, and not long afterward, Checkov dies in an odd accident. While puzzling over what Checkov meant by his strange warning, Ty soon learns that Checkov had lately been given to touting certain horses, telling everyone to back them, and a day or two before the race, the horses would be pulled. As he begins interviewing various people with connections to the Lamplighter Gold Cup for his article, Ty discovers links to the stories he has heard about Bert Checkov's recent activities. The more Ty investigates, the more certain he is that a sinister conspiracy is in place to affect racing odds. He meets a beautiful and sensuous woman, Gail Pominga, who seems somehow involved in the case, and when he lets himself be tempted into an affair with her, he realizes that he may have put himself and his wife into very grave danger indeed. He will need all his courage to ensure not only his safety, but that of his completely helpless wife.

Enquiry (1969)

Jockey Kelly Hughes has been framed for a crime he didn't commit. When his horse Squelch, a heavy favorite, loses the Lemonfizz Crystal Cup race at Oxford, he and trainer Dexter Cranfield are accused of conspiring to lose the race so that another horse trained by Cranfield can win. The Jockey Club Disciplinary Committee holds a board of enquiry, and it is clear to Kelly that the board members are not looking fairly at the evidence since they had made their minds up in advance that he was guilty. Thus both Cranfield and Kelly lose their licenses and are warned off Newmarket Heath. Kelly is determined to find out why he's been framed, especially when Cranfield's beautiful daughter Roberta asks for his help in overcoming her father's suicidal depression. Kelly and Roberta team up to investigate what caused the board members to vote against him, and their sleuthing relationship soon turns into a more personal one. Kelly is a widower, and must learn to let another love into his life. He had always thought that Roberta was a snob like her arrogant and mean father, while she thought he was just another low-class jockey. By getting to know Kelly better, she learns to appreciate people for their worth rather than their pedigree. Kelly runs into plenty of danger while trying to get his license back. Coming back from a dance one night, he feels overwhelmingly dizzy, and unknowingly stops his car on a railroad track and gets out. His car is destroyed by a train, he is injured, and it seems somebody has connected the car heater to the exhaust pipe so that he would be poisoned with carbon monoxide. *Enquiry* is a taut, suspenseful novel, with one of Francis's memorable jockey heroes, and a well-drawn romance between two strong-willed people.

Rat Race (1970)

Matt Shore is a thirty-four-year-old pilot who is "depressed, divorced, [and] broke." He's just started a new job with a small-time firm, Derrydown Sky Taxis, and has moved into a dingy trailer home near the airport. Life is desolate and lonely for him when he is assigned to fly a motley group of passengers to the Haydock racecourse near Liverpool. One of the clients is the famous champion jockey Colin Ross, who invites Matt to watch the races. Matt meets Colin's two sisters, Nancy and Midge, and he and the Rosses get along well together right away. On the trip home, though, the small plane he is flying acts oddly, and Matt makes an emergency landing at an airport near Nottingham. Shortly after everyone disembarks, the plane blows up. On a later trip, the inexperienced pilot, Nancy Ross, has flown her brother Colin to the races on her first solo trip. During the return trip to Cambridge, her radio fails and the fog rolls in, making her plight desperately dangerous since she doesn't know how to land a plane using only instrument controls. Matt follows Nancy, keeps her from getting lost, and assists her in landing safely, thus saving the lives of both Rosses. As Matt investigates, he learns that the incidents involving both his and Nancy's airplanes are not mere accidents, but part of a complex plot designed to wreak maximum injury on innocent victims.

Matt is one of the Francis heroes who changes the most over the course of the book; he is clearly revitalized by having people believe and put their trust in him as a pilot and a friend, and by the love of a good woman. From being completely passive at the outset, he takes the lead in investigating the bombing of his airplane, and his self-confidence grows from there. The flying background in the novel (researched expertly by Mary Francis) is fascinating, and the story itself is highly suspenseful and exciting.

Bonecrack (1971)

Estranged from his father since leaving school, Neil Griffon neverthe-less does what filial duty demands when his father is hospitalized after a car crash. He takes over the running of his father's training stables at Rowley Lodge, presuming it to be a temporary task, until a trainer picked by his father can come in and take over. Neil is attacked and abducted late one night and taken to meet an Italian gangster named Enso Rivera, who has a surprising demand. He wants his son, eighteen-year-old Alessandro, to ride the favorite, Archangel, in the upcoming Derby, because Alessandro had expressed the desire to do so. Whatever Alessandro wants, Enso gives to his only son. Neil knows he cannot risk the reputation of his father's stables, and indeed his father's livelihood, by allowing a relatively inexperienced jockey to ride a horse like Archangel in such an important race. But what can he do? If he doesn't comply, Rivera will destroy his father's life and work. Fig-uring he cannot change the father, Neil sets out to change the son. Capricious, willful, immature, Alessandro (or Alex, as he prefers to be called) fights Neil at every turn, insisting that he be given what his father wants him to have. Slowly, however, Neil shows the young man that he has another choice; he can use his talent to earn what he wants. True success will come only if he works for it. Enso Rivera, who seems unbalanced to begin with, becomes more and more unpre-dictable, until a final act of violence threatens to rob him of the one thing he holds most dear. In a twist of poetic justice, Rivera brings about his own destruction, setting free not only his son, but Neil Griffon as well.

Smokescreen (1972)

In the riveting opening scene of this novel, actor Edward Lincoln is chained to the steering wheel of a car stuck in the desert. He's acting, of course—filming a scene for a movie called *Man in a Car*. The film is being made in Spain, and it's directed by Evan Pentelow, an obstreperous and aggressive man who has little respect for the feelings of actors. "Link," however, is a rare breed of movie actor; he's easygoing, modest, and publicity-shy. He avoids any public knowledge of his private life, and doesn't care that he's a sex symbol to women fans. So far he's not given great performances in the thrillers in which he's been cast, probably due to the fact that he doesn't like showing strong emotions in public. Link has a serene and intelligent wife, Charlie, two energetic and bright sons, and a mentally retarded daughter. As the son of a stable lad, he started out in the movie business as a stunt rider. After completing his part in the film, Link returns to England, only to find that an old family friend, Nerissa Cavesey, is dying of Hodgkin's disease. Nerissa asks Link as a last favor to go to South Africa and find out why her string of racehorses there is not winning any races. The horses' value has dropped enormously, and she doesn't want to leave her nephew and heir, Danilo Cavesey, something worthless when she dies. To oblige her, Link flies to Johannesburg and finds that indeed her horses are not running races up to their capacity. As well as encountering people from the film industry and the usual reporters, he meets Danilo, a golden boy who thinks everything should come easily to him, and Greville Arknold, the shifty trainer of Nerissa's horses. In one of the most dramatic scenes in the novel, Link and several suspects go down a gold mine. Just as they are about to blast with dynamite, someone hits Link on the head with a rock and knocks him out briefly. When he comes to, he's alone in the depths of a dark mine; he can't see anything, but somehow he must find his way out before the dynamite explodes. It's just one incident in an escalating series of events that attend Link's investigations; as he continues to ask questions, the dangerous scenes in which he has acted in the movies begin to look like child's play compared to the reality of the life-threatening situations that he encounters in South Africa.

Slay-Ride (1973)

A talented English steeplechase jockey, Robert (Bob) Sherman, has disappeared in Norway after a race in Oslo, allegedly having stolen a large sum of money from the racecourse. David Cleveland, senior investigator for Britain's Jockey Club, travels to Norway at the request of the Norwegian Jockey Club to investigate the disappearance. In the opening scene, Cleveland and a Norwegian friend and fellow investigator, Arne Kristiansen, are traveling in a small boat along a fjord, about an hour out of Oslo. Kristiansen fears being overheard when he confides in Cleveland, and he has insisted on their isolating themselves in this way to talk about the investigation. Having known the Norwegian for several years, Cleveland agrees, then nearly loses his life when their boat is swamped and he has to swim through freezing water many miles to land. Despite such a disastrous beginning, the investigation continues, and Cleveland begins to make headway. He realizes that it would be very difficult for Sherman to have disappeared with no trace, especially since he was supposed to have taken the day's proceeds from the racecourse, some sixteen thousand kroner in bills and coins, with him. Also in Oslo is Sherman's pregnant wife, Emma, desperate for news of her missing husband and insistent that he wouldn't have stolen the money and run off, leaving her to fend for herself.

Cleveland learns that the missing jockey was always interested in get-rich-quick schemes, and it seems that one of his attempts at making some easy money could have landed him in serious trouble. Was he really attempting to smuggle blue pictures (aka pornography)? Emma Sherman doesn't think so, but the thugs who attack her and ransack her house are obviously looking for something. Cleveland starts tracking whatever it was that Bob Sherman may have been carrying back and forth from England to Norway. Was it something so volatile that it cost Bob Sherman his life?

During his investigation in Norway, Cleveland is assisted not only by a phlegmatic policeman, Knut Lund, but also by Lund's journalist brother, Erik, who has a penchant for big dogs and reckless driving. Erik Lund, with his journalist's nose for information, provides Cleveland with the kind of details about the people involved in his investigation that make the task much easier. Slowly Cleveland is able to zero in on the one person who holds the key to Bob Sherman's disappearance, and in a compelling final scene, he gets at the truth.

Knockdown (1974)

Jonah Dereham is a former prizewinning steeplechase jockey trying to make a living as an honest bloodstock agent. He discovers, however, that staying honest in a business with many temptations for malfeasance may cost him his life. A wealthy American woman, Mrs. Kerry Sanders, comes to him, recommended by American bloodstock agent Pauli Teska, seeking a horse as a gift. She wants to give the horse to young jockey Nicol Brevett, son of her fiancé, wealthy businessman and racing notable Constantine Brevett. But someone doesn't seem to want Mrs. Sanders, nor Jonah on her behalf, to buy the first horse they select, Hearse Puller. After the sales at Ascot, Jonah and Mrs. Sanders are waylaid and forced into signing over ownership of the just-purchased Hearse Puller. Furious and undaunted, Jonah tries a more circuitous path to get Mrs. Sanders the horse she wants. He goes through another bloodstock agent, Ronnie North, to buy the horse River God. He takes precautions to keep River God from being forcibly sold out from under him, but someone makes an attempt to thwart him, thereby causing the accident in which he meets the attractive air traffic controller, Sophie Randolph. Sophie introduces Jonah to her aunt, stud farm owner Mrs. Antonia Huntercombe, who tells Jonah about the pernicious, and illegal, system of kickbacks through which unscrupulous bloodstock owners extort money from owners needing to sell their horses. Jonah, despite threats and violent attempts at coercion, refuses to fall in with the scheme and must find some way of convincing the gang against him that he will not give in. Though the true danger comes from a source he didn't expect, Jonah also finds an ally he hadn't counted on before, when he finally comes to the conclusion of his ordeal.

High Stakes (1975)

Oddly enough, racehorse owners often don't spend much time with their horses. Like many owners, Steven Scott knows little about his horses except that he enjoys watching them run races and win. Steven is an inventor of the popular Rola toys, which have made him a wealthy man. He becomes convinced, however, that his trainer Jody Leeds is systematically cheating him, and he tries to take his horses away from Jody. Jody reacts with total fury, and most of the racing world takes his side and considers Steven to be a fickle, ignorant, and mean-spirited owner. Puzzled by the extremity of Jody's reaction, Steven suspects that more is going on than some garden-variety overcharging of fees, and he is roused to investigate further. Steven also meets Alexandra Ward one day on the street and helps her out of a pickle. They fall in love, and he takes a brief vacation in Miami to be with her. While he is there, he sees a horse for sale who looks amazingly like his star racehorse Energise, and a plan is born. Steven's assistant Owen Idris, his merchant banker friend Charlie Canterfield, Charlie's old friend Bert Huggerneck, and Alexandra all help Steven uncover Jody's secrets and set up an elaborate plot for revenge on him. Jody will be sorry that he ever defrauded the gentle and civilized toymaker Steven Scott.

In the Frame (1976)

Charles Todd is a painter who mostly paints pictures of horses. He regularly goes to stay with his cousin Donald Stuart and his wife Regina for weekends. One day he goes to their house and finds that Regina has been brutally murdered and the house robbed of its antiques, paintings, and a large collection of vintage wine. In the aftermath of this dreadful crime, Donald is completely incapacitated with grief for his beloved and beautiful wife. Charles believes that the only way Donald will be able to go on with his life is if he can find out who killed his wife and why she died so terribly. Donald can't do it for himself, and Charles is determined to help his cousin. At the races, he meets the widowed Maisie Matthews, and learns that her house has just burned down and all its contents are gone. Both Donald and Maisie had recently returned from trips to Australia, and both of them had bought paintings there by the great British horse painter Sir Alfred Munnings. Charles can't believe that this is just a coincidence, so he determines to go to Australia to track down the sellers of these paintings. He uncovers an elaborate scheme of fraud in the painting and selling of fake paintings, especially paintings of horses by masters like Munnings and Herring. Charles enlists the help of his old art school roommate Jik Cassavetes and his wife Sarah to help him with his investigation. Together they set up their own scheme to bring down the fraud ring. *In the Frame* is a fast-moving, suspenseful novel with an exotic and impeccably researched setting.

Risk (1977)

Roland Britten is an accountant by profession, but an amateur jockey by avocation. A junior partner in an accountancy firm in Newbury in Berkshire, he seems to have a nose for uncovering fraud of various sorts. After having won a race, he is kidnapped and taken captive aboard a boat bound for parts unknown. Though the ordeal is harrowing, he manages to escape, with the aid and pluck of a middle-aged schoolmistress, Miss Hilary Margaret Pinlock. She asks only one thing in return, a service that Roland is able to provide, though he is a bit dubious about the wisdom of it. In the long run, however, his friendship with Hilary Pinlock proves to be a wise move. After his escape from his first ordeal, Roland tries to resume business, and life, as usual. Balancing his professional duties and his hopes as an amateur jockey, he digs into the puzzle surrounding his abduction. He has made some enemies in the past by exposing various frauds, and he speculates that one of the men he has helped put in prison might be behind these attempts to put him out of action. A second abduction confirms these suspicions, but he is able to free himself a bit too easily, or so it seems. But a showdown with his nemesis is coming, and a brutal one it proves to be, once Roland finally locates the source of the bitter animosity against him.

Trial Run (1978)

A highly placed official at the Foreign Office seeks the aid of recently retired amateur steeplechase jockey Randall Drew for a sensitive mission to Moscow. There have been vague threats against the life of a young British rider, Lord Johnny Farringford, who has ambitions to be a member of the British team at the 1980 Olympics in Moscow. Randall at first refuses, but then Farringford's brother-in-law, HRH the Prince, a member of the royal family, uses his acquaintance with Randall to urge his cooperation. The threat against young Lord Farringford is amorphous but seems somehow connected with the death of a German rider, Hans Kramer, with whom Lord Farringford had had some association. The Foreign Office is inclined to take a dim view of the whole proceedings, fearing that Randall Drew will only adversely affect British-Soviet relations, but after an attack against Lord Farringford, during which his car is destroyed, Randall Drew accepts the commission. The dead German rider, Kramer, is supposed to have blamed a mysterious Russian named Alyosha from Moscow for his death, and it is Randall's task to uncover Alyosha's identity and discover why he poses a threat to Lord Farringford. During his stay in Moscow, Randall has the assistance of a young British exchange student, Stephen Luce, who serves as a translator, because Randall does not speak any Russian. Randall's patient following of the few clues he has soon yields results when he is viciously attacked following a dinner with several of his British acquaintances in Moscow. He escapes the attempted murder, only to fall prey not much later to another attack in which he is cast into the freezing waters of the Moscow River. Thanks to the intervention of another of his acquaintances, he survives but is soon stricken with the onset of a respiratory infection, one which could prove deadly, due to his susceptibility to bronchitis. Eventually sorting through the maze of misinformation, Randall at last uncovers the terrifying plot and takes steps to see that the plan will not come to fruition when the Olympic Games convene in Moscow.

Whip Hand (1979)

This is the second novel that features Sid Halley, a former steeplechase jockey who is now a racing investigator, and it won both the CWA Gold Dagger Award and the Edgar Award for Best Novel. Sid has his own detective business now, with sidekick Chico Barnes lending a hand as needed. Sid's injured hand has been amputated, and he has been fitted with a high-tech electronic artificial limb. When Rosemary Caspar, a leading trainer's wife, asks Sid to find out why the best horses at their stables aren't winning as expected, he thinks that she is probably making something out of nothing. The Caspar stables had three horses "all top star horses, favorites all winter for the Guineas and the Derby." All of the horses went out to race looking great; all started as favorites, but lost disastrously. All of them were later found to have heart murmurs and had to retire from racing. It begins to look to Sid like something suspicious is happening to the Caspars' horses after all. When horses unexpectedly lose races, it stands to reason that crooked bookies will be making money. Sid's suspicions crystallize when the owner of a large bookmaking firm, Trevor Deansgate, abducts him, puts a shotgun against his good hand, and threatens to shoot it off unless Sid abandons his investigations. Without any hands, Sid would be unable to feed himself or live independently or do much of anything at all. Sid experiences a depth of fear that he's never felt before, and flees to Paris for a few days. But he finds that he can't live with himself as a coward, and returns to continue with his sleuthing. When one of the horses with a heart murmur dies, Sid hires a vet to do a postmortem and finds that the horse has swine erysipelas, a disease usually only found in pigs.

Meanwhile, Sid also has been asked by the head of security for the Jockey Club to look into a possible case of fraud by a top official in the Jockey Club. Horses owned by several syndicates of owners have not been running as expected, and a man who has been warned off race-courses seems to be involved secretly in setting up these syndicates.

In a third subplot, Sid's ex-wife Jenny has been duped by a lover into lending her name and money to a business that turns out to be a fraud. She sends letters that purport to sell high-class furniture polish in order to donate the proceeds to a worthy charity. The lover, Nicholas Ashe, has taken all the proceeds and disappeared. Admiral Roland asks Sid's help in tracking him down so that Jenny can have a better chance of avoiding prosecution.

Jenny's charity is supposedly to help research heart disease; the horses have been given heart disease to stop them winning. Under the direst of threats, Sid has found his courage and his self-respect. In the end, due to one man's courage and integrity, order is restored to the racing world. *Whip Hand*, with its complex, interlacing plots and themes, and its unforgettable characters, is one of the finest of Dick Francis's novels.

Reflex (1980)

Jeremy Folk, a disingenuous young solicitor, appears at Sandown Park racecourse to summon Philip Nore to the bedside of his dying grandmother, Mrs. Lavinia Nore. Mrs. Nore had disowned Philip and his mother when Philip was two, and Philip hasn't seen or spoken to her in the intervening twenty-eight years. Reluctantly persuaded to see the old woman, Philip is shocked to hear that Mrs. Nore wants him to find his younger half sister, Amanda, whom he never knew existed. Mrs. Nore wants to leave her money to Amanda. Philip's first reaction is to refuse, but upon reflection he decides to try to discover the whereabouts of the girl. Philip had a rootless existence as a child, often abandoned by his "butterfly" of a mother, who would leave him for weeks, even months, at a time, with complaisant friends. From one unofficial foster parent, a gay photographer named Charlie, Philip learned the basics of photography. In another home, he became acquainted with horses and racing. Now, at the age of thirty, with the end of his career as a steeplechase jockey looming, Philip begins to realize that his emotionally cold, rootless existence will not be enough to carry him through whatever comes after the point he has to retire from racing. As he searches for Amanda, he begins to grow toward emotional maturity. This is one of the two primary strands of the plot. The other strand involves the events set in motion after the accidental death of a racing photographer, George Millace. Millace is renowned for photos that often catch their subjects in moments of humiliation. A young jockey, the late photographer's son, Steve Millace, asks Philip Nore to accompany him home after he hears that his mother's house has been burgled while they attended his father's funeral. Philip offers his assistance and soon finds himself embroiled in something quite dangerous. Mrs. Millace is brutally attacked in her home by thugs who are intent on finding something belonging to George Millace. While going through some of the seeming rubbish left behind by the burglars, Philip stumbles upon what they were looking for. Though it takes him a while to decipher what George Millace left behind, Philip perseveres, learning more about photography and about his own inner resources. Assisting him along the way are Clare Bergen and Jeremy Folk. When a murderous attack intended for him leaves Folk near death, Philip feels the responsibility and realizes that his old life of emotional distance is over. He ends by carrying on George Millace's unexpected legacy.

Twice Shy (1981)

Jonathan Derry is a physics master and department head at the West Ealing School, possibly in line for a deputy headmastership. He has been married to Sarah for eight years, but their marriage has grown strained over Sarah's wish for the children they have been unable to have. Upon receipt of a distress call from their friends Peter and Donna Keithly, they visit the Keithlys to help them through the aftermath of Donna's disastrous attempt at kidnapping someone else's child. Donna Keithly, like Sarah Derry, is despondent over her childlessness. During the visit, Peter Keithly tells Jonathan about a computer program he has written, based on someone's notes, for handicapping horses. At the last minute, he thrusts some cassette tapes into Jonathan's hands. Jonathan soon discovers that the tapes don't contain music; rather, they contain the computer program Peter has written. When Peter dies in a suspicious accident and Donna and Sarah are held hostage by the vicious Angelo Gilbert, Jonathan realizes he must act quickly in order to protect himself and his wife. Reluctant to turn the program over to Angelo Gilbert, Jonathan concocts a plan to thwart Gilbert and see that it goes to the rightful owner of the program, the widow of Liam O'Rorke. O'Rorke was a professional gambler, and it is his extensive notes that form the basis of the program Peter Keithly wrote. Jonathan is successful in his plan, and he and Sarah move to the United States, where Jonathan takes a teaching position in California.

Fourteen years later, Jonathan's younger brother, horse-mad William, has given up his attempts at a career as a jockey, for he has grown too large to continue to compete successfully. After trying various horse-related jobs, William has taken a position as acting racing manager for the wealthy racing magnate Luke Houston. Happily cohabiting with the enticing Cassie Morris, William is wondering whether he's really ready at last to settle down. But violence erupts on his very doorstep when Angelo Gilbert reappears, looking for the Derry who did him out of the computer program fourteen years before. To protect himself and Cassie from the reckless Angelo, William has to delve into the secrets of the computer program and seek out Angelo's father, Harry Gilbert, in order to bring the violence to an end once and for all.

Banker (1982)

The Paul Ekaterin merchant bank in the city of London was founded generations ago by the Ekaterin family. However, the youngest representative of the family, Tim Ekaterin, has started at the bottom and worked hard to establish himself on his own merits in the bank. He loves banking and has a real talent for it. His boss is Gordon Michaels, an older man married to Judith, a much younger second wife. Tim is hopelessly in love with Judith, but he won't do anything about it because she is married and he respects both Gordon and the institution of marriage. In the memorable opening scene of the novel, Tim sees Gordon standing confusedly in the fountain outside their building. He rescues him and gets him to a doctor. It seems that Gordon doesn't want anyone to know that he has Parkinson's disease, but he has recently switched medications, causing hallucinations. Gordon goes on a medical leave, and Tim takes over his job in the interim. When Oliver Knowles applies to the bank for a loan in order to buy a champion racing stallion, Sandcastle, for his breeding farm, some of the older bankers are highly dubious. The bank has never loaned five million pounds for a racehorse before, but Tim endorses the loan, and they go ahead. The horse seems to be a successful breeder, but when the first crop of foals are born, many of them have serious birth defects; they are born without hooves or an eye, or with deformed legs. This devastates the hopes of breeding Sandcastle successfully, and the bank is in danger of losing a great deal of money on a bad loan. When Tim goes out to look into this problem at the stud farm one day, he finds that Oliver's charming and intelligent teenage daughter, Ginnie, has been brutally killed. Tim had become close to Ginnie in a brotherly way, and her death is the first event in his life that moves him from cheerful innocence to an awareness of tragedy and emotional pain. Tim is impelled to find out who has killed Ginnie and jeopardized his career. *Banker* has one of Dick Francis's most complex and fascinating plots, and the emotional impact of the story is particularly strong.

The Danger (1983)

Liberty Market is a firm that quietly helps kidnap victims return alive from their ordeals. Andrew Douglas is a former insurance agent with Lloyds of London, who is now one of the partners in Liberty Market. Most of the other partners and associates are either ex-SAS or Army men, so he is rather the odd man out. Many people think that Andrew is emotionally cold; he thinks he is merely a logical man. But he is experienced and wise in understanding the psychology of kidnappers and the effect of being kidnapped on the victims, and so he is sent to Italy when Alessia Cenci, one of Europe's foremost female jockeys, is snatched from her home. Andrew helps her father Paolo through the process, and negotiates with the kidnappers. He recovers Alessia, but she is emotionally damaged by her experience, and goes to England to stay with an old friend for security. She and Andrew continue to see each other, and a strong bond forms between them. Andrew is a fairly typical Francis hero in that he is prone to concealing his feelings, although he has strong ones. He behaves decently to everyone except the villains, on whom he is suitably tough. In the second part of the novel, a little boy named Dominic Nerrity is stolen from his mother while playing at the beach. Andrew and Alessia are together when this kidnapping is reported, and she insists on using her own personal comprehension of what it's like to be kidnapped in order to help the distraught mother. Andrew and his colleague Tony Vine discover that this kidnapping is linked to the racing world too; Dominic's father owns a very valuable horse that has recently won the Derby. Clearly a serial kidnapper is targeting victims from the racing world. In the third part of the novel, Alessia has recovered enough to travel to Washington, D.C., to ride the great Italian racehorse Brunelleschi in a festive international race. Unfortunately, the kidnapper strikes again, and this time he nabs Morgan Freemantle, the senior steward of the Jockey Club, who is also in Washington for the race. Andrew is sent out to attempt once more to find the elusive kidnapper and recover his latest victim, but everything goes very wrong for him, and the novel climaxes with a surprise twist sure to keep any reader up late at night.

Proof (1984)

Tony Beach is a recent widower who owns a wine shop in a small town near the Thames River in Berkshire. Racehorse trainers Jack and Flora Hawthorn are Tony's clients and friends, and when they throw a big party for their racing friends, Tony is asked to attend and provide the liquor. The party turns into a shambles when the brakes on a horse van fail, and the van rolls downhill and careens into a party tent full of guests, including an Arab sheik. Tony helps both the police and the Hawthorns in the dreadful aftermath of the incident, and his specialized knowledge draws him, willy-nilly, into the official investigation. It seems that just before the van crash, one of the guests had told Tony that he thought a nearby restaurant was passing cheap liquor off as expensive brands. Tony has an unusual skill; he has a nose for telling one wine or whisky from another simply by smelling and tasting them. The police ask for his help in investigating this fraud, which could be linked to the incident at the Hawthorns' party, and he goes willingly with them to test samples in pubs and restaurants. He doesn't realize what he's getting into, and what seems like an investigation of minor fraud turns into a case of murder, intimidation, and large-scale thievery. But at least his detective work distracts Tony from his mourning for a while, and, in the great tradition of Francis heroes, this unlikely detective shows hidden depths of courage and shrewdness when challenged with danger.

Break In (1985)

Successful jockey Kit Fielding has an almost telepathic ability to communicate with the horses he rides, and he once shared that ability with his twin sister Holly, at least until her marriage. Holly is married to Bobby Allardeck, scion of a family that the Fielding twins had been taught from an early age to despise and distrust. When a scandal sheet starts printing damaging stories about Bobby Allardeck's stables, stories which could ruin him completely, Holly calls on her brother for help. Kit has to win Bobby's trust and overcome the prejudices of generations of Fieldings in order to accomplish the task, but he can't abandon his sister in such a time of dire need. Kit can't understand why Bobby himself should be the target of such an attack, and soon the trails lead to Bobby's obnoxious father, business tycoon Maynard Allardeck. Maynard has some powerful enemies who will seemingly stop at nothing to get at him, and Kit must find a solution that will neutralize not only the nasty Maynard, but his enemies as well. Along the way he encounters the beautiful Danielle de Brescou, niece by marriage of the royal Princess Casilia de Brescou for whom he rides. The race is on to win the heart of the woman he loves and to save his sister and her husband.

Bolt (1986)

Troubled by Danielle de Brescou's sudden seeming disinterest in him, Kit Fielding continues to ride for her aunt-by-marriage, the Princess

Casilia de Brescou. When a power-mad French businessman threatens the princess's husband, the elderly and ailing M. de Brescou, the princess calls upon Kit to help her family withstand the onslaught. Henri Nanterre is the heir to his family's share in the firm of de Brescou and Nanterre, and he has decided it is time for the business to strike out in a very profitable new venture, the manufacture and export of arms. Roland de Brescou finds the idea repugnant and wants no part of it, but for Nanterre to be able to obtain the necessary license, he needs the de Brescou name on the deal. When de Brescou refuses to cooperate, Nanterre warns of violent consequences. Soon after, two of the Princess Casilia's racehorses are found murdered in their stalls, the victims of a so-called humane killer known as the "bolt." Once again Kit is racing against time, trying to find a way to neutralize the vicious Nanterre and stop the killing of the princess's horses, while at the same time keeping his old nemesis, Maynard Allardeck, from causing any more trouble.

Hot Money (1987)

Malcolm Pembroke is a wealthy gold trader with a penchant for marrying and producing offspring. When his fifth wife, the grasping Moira, is murdered in her greenhouse, Malcolm suspects that he himself is the ultimate target. Suspicious that a member of the family means him harm, he turns to his third son, Ian, a fairly successful amateur steeplechase jockey, for protection. He also entrusts Ian with the task of figuring out which member of the extended family of ex-wives and half siblings most wants him out of the way. Ian, the only member of the family who seems to love his father unreservedly, is a bit reluctant to take on the job, but he welcomes the chance to mend a breach with his father, caused by marriage to the odious (and unlamented) gold-digging Moira. With the aid of private investigator Norman West, Ian begins delving into the family's past, trying to sort out the reasons why a member of the Pembroke clan would resort to murder to get what he or she wants most, access to Malcolm Pembroke's vast wealth. As Ian and his father grow closer, the rest of the family seem determined to close ranks against them, fearing that Ian's only motive in assisting Malcolm is to become sole heir to his fortune. Slowly, however, Ian chips away at decades of mistrust and jealousy to get at the root of the problem. In an explosive climax, Ian identifies the killer and brings the family closer than ever before, with a real chance for healing and happiness.

The Edge (1988)

Tor Kelsey is an independently wealthy young man who has traveled all over the world, and recently returned home to England. He had been brought up as very much a part of the racing scene by an aunt who adored racing, but he's been away from England for most of his adult life, so nobody recognizes him. The Jockey Club Security Service discovers this valuable combination of anonymity and racing knowledge and recruits Tor to be their undercover man on racecourses, looking for fraud and crime. He uses a variety of disguises, and, chameleon-like, can fit in anywhere. He loves the challenge of it all, and accepts readily when he is asked to go after Julius Apollo Filmer, a rich, shrewd megalomaniac who has caused a great deal of disturbance in the British racing world. Because he intimidated a witness, Filmer has recently managed to be acquitted of murdering a stable lad, but Tor and his colleagues are convinced of his guilt. The chances are excellent that he will strike again and do further damage to racing. The Jockey Club finds that Filmer has bought a half interest in one of the horses traveling across Canada on the Great Transcontinental Mystery Racing Train, so that he can get on the train as an owner. Both the British and Canadian Jockey Clubs believe that he will try some mischief while on board, if only to get revenge against the racing authorities for trying to warn him off racecourses. Tor joins the train as part of a troupe of actors who are going to put on a mystery play while the race train travels from Ottawa to Vancouver. He pretends to be an actor who is pretending to be a waiter, using an alias of Tommy Titmuss to preserve his undercover status. As an actor-waiter, Tor mixes easily with the staff, observes the activities of the passengers, and carries out a relentless campaign against the nefarious plotting of the evil Filmer. *The Edge* is very much in the mode of a classic suspense tale, and a good deal of emphasis is placed on lively characterization and the dramatic Canadian settings.

Straight (1989)

Derek Franklin, a successful steeplechase jockey, has recently been injured. He receives word that his older brother, Greville, has been injured, and upon arrival at the hospital, he discovers that his brother will not survive his injuries. Upon Greville's death, Derek inherits responsibility for Greville's successful gemstone import business. Struggling to learn the ropes of a business completely alien to him, Derek slowly becomes acquainted with the facts of his brother's life. Greville was nineteen years older than Derek, and the two were friendly, meeting at most two or three times a year, but were never particularly close. The more Derek learns about his brother, his business, and his life, the more he regrets the lost opportunities. He very quickly learns that, not long before his death, Greville had taken out a large loan in order to buy some uncut diamonds. The diamonds, however, have disappeared, leaving Greville's business in a difficult position. As Derek searches for the missing diamonds, he becomes aware that someone else is after them as well. Greville loved gadgets, and he also loved secrecy, and Derek has to use all his ingenuity to follow the pathways of his brother's sometimes devious thought processes in order to unlock all of the elder Franklin's secrets. Complicating the situation is contention over one of Greville's investments, a racehorse named Dozen Roses. The horse's trainer, Nicholas Loder, is after Derek to sell the horse, but Derek resists. He suspects Loder of trying to put something over on him, but he's not quite sure just what it is that Loder is trying to do. Derek finds himself attracted to Greville's mistress, a beautiful married woman named Clarissa Williams. Though their first meeting is far from cordial, Derek is rapidly able to understand the depth of his brother's attraction to her. Eventually, Derek sorts through all the puzzles surrounding his brother's life, business, and death, growing closer in death to his brother than he ever was in life.

Longshot (1990)

John Kendall is thirty-two, and he is on the brink of becoming a successful writer. Kendall has been working on creating and leading adventure trips for a travel agency, and has translated his knowledge of survival techniques into several guidebooks on how to survive in the Arctic, the jungle, and other inhospitable places. Now he wants to try writing fiction. As the novel opens, he has quit his day job and is freezing in a garret while trying to write a novel. His first novel has been accepted, but it's not yet published. Kendall is tremendously excited about becoming a published novelist, and especially about the news that an American publisher will publish his book too. But it's a very cold winter, he has no heat, and he is offered the chance to stay somewhere warm for a few weeks while working on a commissioned biography of a racehorse trainer, Tremayne Vickers. Kendall accepts the job and goes to stay at Tremayne's country house and stables in Berkshire. Tremayne's daughter-in-law Mackie and some of the neighbors pick Kendall up at the train station on his first day, and their jeep slides into an icy ditch on the way home. Kendall promptly uses his knowledge of survival techniques to save their lives, and this incident seals his acceptance as an integral part of the Vickers household. When one of the former stable lads is found murdered, Kendall is pulled inevitably into the investigation and its consequent disruption of the lives of the Vickers family and their friends. *Longshot* is as much a classic murder mystery as a thriller. The sincerity and charm of Francis's writing comes through strongly, and it's fascinating to read about Kendall's progression from nonfiction to fiction writer, which seems to echo closely Dick Francis's own career.

Comeback (1991)

A career diplomat in the Foreign Service, Peter Darwin (no relation to Charles) is on his way to England from his latest posting for a bit of a vacation before starting a new job in London. He stops briefly in Miami, where he looks up a colleague, Fred Hutchings, who is now the British consul in Miami. Fred asks him to help two friends of his, Vicky Larch and her husband Greg Wayfield, who are about to depart for Gloucestershire to attend Vicky's daughter's wedding. Darwin reluctantly agrees, but after Vicky and Greg are viciously mugged outside a restaurant in Miami, he finds his assistance even more welcome than before. He travels with Vicky and Greg to the Cheltenham area, where he grew up before his mother married diplomat John Darwin. Peter hopes to be able to leave Vicky and Greg in the capable, if not overly welcoming, hands of Belinda Larch, but disaster strikes in the form of a fire at the veterinary practice where Ken McClure, Belinda's fiancé, is a partner and highly respected equine surgeon. Peter does what he can to help, and he discovers that Ken is in danger of losing his reputation after several horses under his care have died, for seemingly no reason, after what appeared to have been successful surgeries.

Peter very quickly senses some sort of conspiracy, and when a body is discovered in the aftermath of the fire, he is even more convinced that something nefarious is afoot. He witnesses one of Ken's operations, during which nothing goes wrong, and he is convinced that Ken is a deliberate target. Following a meager trail of evidence, Peter uses all the skills he's ever learned as a diplomat to get at the root of the conspiracy that seems aimed at destroying not only Ken McClure but the entire veterinary practice. The trail leads Peter back into his own childhood, and a tragedy that has cast very long shadows into the present.

Driving Force (1992)

A retired jockey who runs his own horse transport business, Freddie Croft lives and works in Pixhill, "a big village verging on small town sprawling across a fold of downland in Hampshire, south of Newbury." Croft Raceways transports horses to races, sends broodmares to stud farms, and brings foreign-bought racehorses to English stables. Freddie has fourteen vans "zigzagging round England most days carrying multimillion fortunes on the hoof." Against all of Freddie's strict rules, two of his drivers, Brett Gardner and Dave Yates, pick up a hitchhiker one night and then find him dead in the van the next time they stop. After the corpse is removed, Freddie sees a shadowy figure searching the van late at night. Then Jogger, his mechanic, finds a hidden metal box (a "stranger") attached to the underside of one of the other horse vans. Are the van drivers smuggling drugs? When Jogger is found dead in an inspection pit, Freddie knows for certain that something deadly is happening in his vans. Just before his death, Jogger had left Freddie a message on his answering machine, but it's in Jogger's own personal version of cockney rhyming slang, and Freddie can't figure out what he's saying. Francis has produced an ingenious plot, an unguessable solution, and a likable and competent hero surrounded by interesting secondary characters.

Decider (1993)

Lee Morris is an architect who makes a living and supports his family by restoring old ruins and turning them into unusual and beautiful homes. Lee married Amanda at a very young age, and now they have six sons, whom he adores. His sons all have quite different natures, from the shy Neil to the mature and responsible Christopher. Lee's marriage is not happy, but he has stayed in it for the sake of his children. His late mother had made a bad first marriage, to Keith Stratton, who beat and raped her. She ran away and divorced him, and made an excellent second marriage to the man who fathered Lee. In order to hush her up about his son's violence, Keith's father, Lord Stratton, gave her some shares in the family business, the Stratton Park racecourse. He also paid for Lee's education. When Lord Stratton dies, Lee feels a sense of obligation and for the first time goes to a racecourse shareholder's meeting. There he meets the eccentric and very rich Stratton family, who have clearly hated both him and the memory of his mother for years. Some of the Strattons want to keep their troubled racecourse going and even improve it; some want to sell the land to developers. Because of his crucial shares, Lee gets involved, much to his dismay, in the shenanigans of this often violent and fractious family. Lee is naturally decisive (except about his marriage, perhaps) and his presence acts as a synthesis for action, and sometimes brutality, on the part of the family members. *Decider* has a fast-moving, complex plot, with lashings of violence and well-developed characters, but it also has one of Dick Francis's finest portraits of the joys of family life.

Wild Horses (1994)

Rising young director Thomas Lyon and his film crew are on location in Newmarket, filming a movie based on a scandal that had rocked the racing world some twenty-six years ago. Sonia Wells, the wife of young trainer Jackson Wells, had been found hanged in the stables. Though foul play was suspected, no one was ever indicted for the crime. Howard Tyler, a highly successful novelist and Oscar-winning screenwriter, penned a novel based on the story and has adapted the book for the movie. He is not pleased with some of the changes that Thomas Lyon has wrought upon his creation, and he complains to his friend Alison Visborough, the niece of Sonia Wells. Alison leaks word of Howard Tyler's unhappiness to the media, and the resulting publicity almost costs Thomas Lyon his job. Alison Visborough and her family are very unhappy that the film is even being made, fearing that it will damage the reputation of her late father, Rupert Visborough, who gave up his political aspirations after the scandal surrounding his sister-in-law's death.

Thomas Lyon not only has to deal with potential disaster on the movie set, he is also confronted by the strange legacy from an old friend, racing journalist Valentine Clark, whose dying words land Thomas right smack in the middle of a mystery. Clark has left his library to Thomas, but someone else seems determined to have it, attacking Clark's elderly sister and putting her in hospital with severe wounds. What did Clark's cryptic last words really mean? And how was he connected with the mystery of Sonia Wells's death? Thomas Lyon determines that he must, if possible, get to the truth of what really happened to Sonia Wells, not only to provide a proper ending for his movie, but to stop the escalating violence surrounding him and others involved in the making of the movie *Unstable Times*.

Come to Grief (1995)

In the third Sid Halley novel, Sid knows who the villain is very early on, but he can hardly believe it himself, and everyone else thinks he's crazy for suspecting such a popular, kindly man. It seems that some sick individual is going around the peaceful English countryside in the middle of the night and cutting the hooves off innocent horses. Sid is asked by the mother of Rachel Ferns, a girl dying of leukemia, to help find out who mutilated her beloved pony Silverboy. Sid becomes good friends with Rachel; the crippled man and the dying child share an indomitable courage under adversity. As he investigates, it becomes clear that one man was present on each occasion when a horse was attacked. That man is Sid's good friend Ellis Quint, a former amateur jockey and now a famous television personality. Ellis even recorded a heart-wrenching television show with Rachel Ferns right after her pony was destroyed, so it seems that he had committed the dreadful act in order to improve his ratings. Sid knows that Ellis is guilty; Ellis even hints to Sid that he can't help doing it—it's a compulsion for him. But when Ellis is arrested, the great British public is angry with Sid for making such lethal allegations against a vastly popular icon of British life. As the book opens, Ellis is on trial, and his father is so upset that he tries to kill Sid and succeeds in breaking his arm. There's a vicious campaign against Sid in the tabloid press, so he's not getting many investigative jobs. Sid is constantly attacked by the sleazy tabloid newspaper *The Pump*. India Cathcart, one of their columnists, assails him almost daily in print—but is she writing the pieces herself or is somebody behind the scenes orchestrating the destruction of Sid's reputation and his business? It's a fascinating story about the nature of celebrity and how the media can make or destroy people.

To the Hilt (1996)

Courage under adversity is certainly one of the recurring themes in Dick Francis's novels. That human quality is a strongly evoked motif in *To the Hilt*. The hero is Alexander Kinloch, who lives in the Monadhliath Mountains in Scotland. He is a painter, especially of golfers and golf courses, but what he really paints is "the perseverance of the human spirit"—including courage in the face of trouble, and the courage to succeed in a difficult undertaking. In the opening scene of the novel, Al is attacked outside the front door of his cottage by four beefy toughs who keep demanding to know, "Where is it?" They never tell him what "it" is, and throw him down the mountainside when he refuses to tell them anything. Alexander gets word that his stepfather, Sir Ivan Westering, has had a heart attack, and he immediately travels down to London to help his mother and stepfather. Sir Ivan tells him that the finance director of his business, the King Alfred Brewery, has embezzled all of the firm's money and disappeared. The stress has brought on Sir Ivan's heart attack. Al and his mother both want to keep the gentle and civilized Sir Ivan from suffering any more stress, so Al agrees to take on a power of attorney and look into getting the brewery's affairs back on track. He does a brilliant job of it, helped out by the usual fascinating Francis secondary characters, but Sir Ivan's daughter Patsy and son-in-law Surtees Benchmark continually attempt to block his efforts and try to threaten him physically. Sir Ivan also asks Al to hide two of his treasured possessions: the King Alfred Gold Cup, a medieval chalice, and his prizewinning racehorse, Golden Malt, in order to keep them away from his creditors. This effort is complicated by the fact that Golden Malt is trained by Al's estranged wife, Emily Cox. (One of the most erotic love scenes in a Francis novel is here, when Al and Emily unexpectedly make love one night. It's clear that they still love each other, even though they are completely unable to live with each other.) Al's uncle, the Earl of Kinloch, also trusts him completely and has asked him to hide the hilt of Bonnie Prince Charlie's sword away from zealous historians who believe that such a priceless artifact rightfully belongs to the state rather than a private family. Dr. Zoe Lang, a retired professor and expert on Scottish history, is one such zealot. She is relentless in her desire to find the hilt and turn it over to the nation as a national historic treasure, while Al has an irresistible urge to paint her ageless spirit. When he paints her portrait, he depicts the young and passionate woman lying just underneath the elderly exterior. "I wanted to paint her as young, vibrant, fanatical, with the ghost of the way she looked now superimposed in thin light gray lines, like age's cobwebs." It's his best painting yet, and a suitable subject for the painter who can hide anything valuable—except his own talent and courage.

10 Lb. Penalty (1997)

Benedict Juliard, a few weeks shy of his eighteenth birthday, would happily remain in training to become a jockey, but his father, wealthy businessman George Juliard, has other plans for his son. When Ben is dismissed from his position at the stables of Sir Vivian Durridge on trumped-up charges of glue-sniffing, he is whisked immediately to Brighton to see his father. The widowed elder Juliard, in his late thirties, is wealthy and successful, but he has decided to follow his inclinations for a political career. He has been asked to stand for election to Parliament, and he wants Ben, his only family, to be at his side during the campaign. Though Ben and his father are somewhat estranged, he accedes to his father's wishes and begins to act as a bodyguard and driver for his father while learning the ins and outs of campaigning for office. Ben hasn't been long at his father's side when someone attempts to shoot George Juliard. Thereafter Ben is determined to stick by his father's side and keep him safe from harm. But who, Ben wonders, would rather see George Juliard dead than elected to Parliament? Orinda Nagle, widow of the late MP, Dennis Nagle, had hopes of being selected to run for the seat herself, but she has been passed over by the selection committee. Paul Bethune, the opposing candidate, has a shaky reputation, being a proponent of family values who has been publicly exposed as an adulterer. Alderney Wyvern, Orinda Nagle's constant escort and the late Dennis Nagle's best friend, is not happy with George Juliard's candidacy, but could he be behind the attempts on the elder Juliard's life? A muckraking journalist, Usher Rudd, seems determined to find something distasteful in Juliard's past, even going so far as to intimate that Ben and George are not father and son, but lovers instead. Ben matures quickly as he and his father, for the first time in their lives, begin to develop a close relationship. As George Juliard ascends the political ladder toward his ultimate goal, the prime ministership, Ben goes to university, attains a very respectable degree, and finds a job in the insurance industry. All the while, however, George Juliard's nemesis lurks in the background. Can Ben save his father, and himself, by finally trapping the would-be killer?

Second Wind (1999)

Perry Stuart has a Ph.D. in physics and works as a meteorologist for BBC television. His colleague and friend at the BBC weather center is Kris Ironside, who suffers from manic depression and an intermittent desire to commit suicide. Kris is a weekend pilot with his own Piper Cherokee. They are "both single, both 31," and have devoted sets of fans. "Small groups of the great wide public with special needs tended to gravitate to particular forecasters . . . Landowners, great and small, felt comfortable with Kris," while Perry's followers tend to be involved with horses.

When Kris flies them to a Sunday lunch in Newmarket with some fans who have become acquaintances, they take the first steps on a course that will pitch them into the middle of a dark conspiracy that will threaten both their lives. Caspar Harvey, their host, introduces them to Robin Darcy from Florida. The manic Kris has always wanted to fly through the eye of a hurricane; Robin offers him the opportunity and the plane to do so, as long as he makes a detour to a tiny unoccupied Caribbean island called Trox. Kris flies to Florida during hurricane season, and persuades Perry to join him. When Hurricane Odin forms, Kris is ready to go—but he doesn't tell Perry about the side trip to Trox Island until they're ready to leave and Perry is navigating. Oddly enough, they find nothing on Trox but a herd of cattle and some abandoned buildings. They make it into the eye of the hurricane, and it's an amazing, overwhelming experience for both of them. The trouble comes when they try to fly through the "second wind" on the other side of the eye. The plane goes down, and Perry is flung into the sea in his life preserver. He is a very strong swimmer and surfer, so somehow he is able to survive a night in a hurricane on the open sea, and the current takes him into the cliffs of Trox Island. He has to wait several days for rescue, and while he waits he drinks milk from the cows and finds a concealed safe with a mysterious list in multiple languages and a Geiger counter locked away in it. Rescue comes in the form of a planeload of menacing figures in radiation suits, carrying machine guns. They blindfold him and eventually release him on Grand Cayman. Perry is alarmed by this show of force, and takes his story to two quiet men in an unobtrusive government department in London. They persuade Perry to help them discover what's going on at Trox Island, but finding all the truth of this complex matter becomes a dangerous exercise for Perry and Kris.

Shattered (2000)

Professional jockey Martin Stukely dies in a steeplechase accident at Cheltenham, after arranging for his good friend Gerard Logan to receive a mysterious package. The package is delivered to Gerard's glassblowing shop in a small tourist village in the Cotswolds on New Year's Eve 1999. As the celebrations to ring in a new millennium occupy the inhabitants of the village, Gerard's shop is burgled and the package is stolen. In the package is a videotape, and it turns out that other tapes owned by Martin are stolen the next day. Thus begins a complex tale of murder, extortion, and theft revolving around the struggle for possession of a vital medical discovery. Gerard falls in love with Detective Constable Catherine Dodd, but works on his own to untangle the mystery, in spite of the predations of a murderous mob of venal bookmakers. With the assistance of a young computer hacker, a muscle-bound chauffeur, and an ex-con, Gerard follows the trails of several different videotapes to a violent resolution in which the police have a role after all. Throughout the story, Gerard's mastery of glassmaking is integrated into the plot as a key element.

FIELD OF THIRTEEN

Published in 1998, this is the first collection of Dick Francis's own short stories. Eight of the stories were previously published elsewhere; five were written expressly for this book.

"Raid at Kingdom Hill"

Tricksy Wilcox, a gent who "at thirty-four had brought unemployment to a fine art," had a bright idea one day to make money at Kingdom Hill Racecourse. Trouble is, Tricksy is not the most intelligent of men. When someone phones in a bomb threat at Kingdom Hill, Tricksy thinks to scoop up lots of free cash. Major Kevin Cawdor-Jones, manager of the racecourse, is worried about the expenses of making the whole venue more secure. When the bomb threat is called in, his worst nightmare comes true.

As Dick Francis notes in his introduction to the story, a bomb threat at a racecourse was pure fiction when he wrote the story, but years later a bomb scare halted the running of the 1997 Grand National Steeplechase at Aintree.

"Dead on Red"

Professional assassin Emil Jacques Guirlande is afraid of flying. Thus, in order to carry out his commission to murder beloved English jockey Red Millbrook, he must drive to England, taking a ferry across to bring his car to England. Gypsy Joe Smith, the trainer for whom Red Millbrook had achieved stunning success, is determined to root out the jockey's killer. The murder seems motiveless, though Smith's second-string jockey, Davey Rockman, swaggering ladies' man, has much to gain from the death.

In several twists of poetic justice, the guilty reap what they have sown in particularly appropriate ways.

"Song for Mona"

Joanie Vine is desperately ashamed of her mother, Mona Watkins, a Welshwoman who makes a living looking after horses. The social-climbing Joanie does her best to distance herself and her snooty husband, auctioneer Peregrine Vine, from Mona, and Mona generously overlooks her daughter's snobbishness. Mona finds a job, and a warm and inviting home, with aristocratic, gold medal–winning rider Oliver Bolingbroke and his American country music star wife, Cassidy Lovelace Ward. They, at least, have the sense to appreciate Mona for herself. But when tragedy strikes, the payback for past malice proves to be steep indeed.

"Bright White Star"

A couple desperate to get their training stables off to a good start pull a clever switch, whereby they get a Thoroughbred colt for very little investment. But their lack of kindness when dealing with a tramp costs them very dear in the end. The message in this story is definitely a variation of the Golden Rule: Do nasty unto others, and you'll get what's coming to you.

"Collision Course"

What happens when a gifted newspaper editor, suddenly out of a job, finds himself rudely treated at a posh restaurant? Bill Williams gets the cold shoulder just because he arrived at the riverside restaurant in a boat. Add to that a brash self-promoter who needs all the good publicity he can get, and the stage is set for a serious comeuppance. Never underestimate the power of the press—or a seriously annoyed man who has a gift for invective.

"Nightmare"

Martin Retsov had, for three years at least, abandoned his chosen profession after the death of his father. That death still haunts him, but he has finally worked up his nerve to work an old dodge: stealing a broodmare and her unborn foal. But, just when you least expect it, there can be a joker in the deck, as Martin Retsov is about to find out.

"Carrot for a Chestnut"

Young jockey Chick has a grudge against the world; he never gets his due, everyone somehow slights him, nothing ever goes quite the way it should for him. When someone bribes him to slip a carrot to a particular chestnut, he's willing. Trouble is, he's two hours late in giving the carrot to the horse. He keeps assuring himself that it doesn't matter, but when disaster strikes, thanks to his inability to follow instructions, he somehow manages to shift the blame—as usual. But fate has a bit of poetic justice in store for Chick. And Dick Francis provides a clever twist at the end, to surprise even the most alert reader.

"The Gift"

Fred Collyer was once a gifted, highly respected journalist. He still has flashes of the old brilliance, but mostly they're dulled now by his taste for alcohol. He's just been given his last chance by his editor, if he only knew it, and just when he needs it most, a blockbuster story is within his grasp. Someone is planning to work a big scam at the Kentucky Derby, and Fred has received a scoop by being in the right place at the right time. But can he make use of "the gift" and resurrect his career? You'll have to read the story to see just how it turns out.

"Spring Fever"

Angela Hart, plump, motherly, and fifty-two, falls in love with her jockey, young, muscular, and twenty-four. Making decisions under the influence of love can be disastrous, but will Angela Hart learn that not everyone can be trusted at face value before it's too late?

"Blind Chance"

Arnold Roper has a good fiddle going, employing quite a few other men to help him make money with his surefire betting system. He sees no reason that the system should ever be detected, and he can go on making money for as long as he likes. But factor in a young blind man with a transistor radio tuned to a low frequency and a betting shop owner in the right place at the right time, and things could get dicey. Once again, Dick Francis serves up a clever twist, right at the end.

"Corkscrew"

Doing good is a good thing, right? But sometimes kindness can get you in all sorts of trouble. Jules Reginald Harlow helps out a distressed Englishwoman from impulse and then finds himself cheated by a slick lawyer who doesn't care whom he defrauds as long as he can get away with it. But the slick lawyer just happened to pick on a very wealthy man to whom the principles of justice are exceedingly important. Once again, what goes around, comes around.

"The Day of the Losers"

Austin Dartmouth Glenn heads out to the Grand National with a thick wad of banknotes—notes he was supposed to sit on for five years before spending them—the rewards of a particularly vicious bank robbery. Jerry Springwood is a jockey who has lost his nerve but who has the chance to win the Grand National, if he can only hang on long enough. Who will win, and who will lose, on this day at the Grand National? Dick Francis has some very interesting answers to these questions.

"Haig's Death"

At forty-two Christopher Haig wishes he had had a more adventurous life, and when he sets out one day to perform his duties as a judge at the Winchester Spring Meeting, he has little idea that this day will be his last. One might not think that the death of a judge at a racecourse could have quite such an effect on many people's lives, but Dick Francis shows us just how complex a world a racecourse is and the many and varied people whose lives are closely intertwined with just a single race.

CAST OF CHARACTERS

Dick Francis rarely uses series characters (Sid Halley is a notable exception), so each book is full of new people who are often memorable and fascinating. Some critics have thought that the villains often have aristocratic-sounding names, but all we conclude is that it may be best not to have a name that begins with *Q!*

Abbott, Norris (*Whip Hand*). Perhaps the real name of Nicholas Ashe, Jenny Halley's crooked boyfriend.

Adams, Annette (*Straight*). As the personal assistant to Greville Franklin, she is very capable at her job, though apparently incapable of making significant decisions without the guidance of someone senior.

Adams, Paul J. (*For Kicks*). Wealthy owner of a number of racehorses who has a reputation for malicious violence; an associate of trainer Hedley Humber.

Akkerton, Vince (*Twice Shy*). Employee of a business in Newmarket that mass-produces food. A coworker of Chris Norwood's, he is able to help Jonathan Derry obtain some important information about Norwood.

Alec (*Banker*). A colleague of Tim Ekaterin's at the bank. He is lively and sardonic, and Tim enjoys working with him very much.

Alexis, Mrs. (*Proof*). A plump and jolly pub owner who helps Tony Beach uncover fraud in the liquor trade.

Alfie (*Straight*). Older bloke knowledgeable about racing who packs up the orders at Saxony Franklin.

Allardeck, Holly Fielding (*Bolt; Break In*). Sister of Kit Fielding, wife of Bobby Allardeck. She assists her husband in running a training stables.

Allardeck, Maynard (*Bolt; Break In*). A ruthless businessman who yearns for the prestige of a peerage, he hates the Fielding family and cannot forgive his son for having committed the ultimate betrayal by marrying Holly Fielding.

Allardeck, Robertson, aka Bobby (*Bolt; Break In*). Husband of Holly Fielding and brother-in-law to Kit, he belongs to a family who have been deadly enemies of the Fielding clan for generations.

Alnutt, Mrs. (*For Kicks*). "Round, cheerful little person" who looks after the unmarried lads in the Earl of October's stables.

Alyosha (*Trial Run*). A diminutive form of the Russian name Alexei.

The mysterious Alyosha seems to be at the heart of the conspiracy that brings Randall Drew to Moscow. The question is, who (or perhaps, what) is Alyosha?

Amberezzio, Phillip ("The Gift," *Field of Thirteen*). A straight jockey, he is an unwitting part of Marius Tollman's scheme to alter the fair running of the Kentucky Derby.

Ambrose, John, aka Brose (*Comeback*). Deputy director of the Security Service for the British Jockey Club. After an introduction via Annabel Nutbourne, he provides Peter Darwin with some very interesting information on the insuring of racehorses.

Amhurst, Lucy (*Comeback*). One of the partners in Carey Hewett's veterinary practice in Cheltenham. She is chiefly a small-animal vet, with expertise in sheep and ponies as well.

Andrews, Thomas (*Odds Against*). He is a small-time crook who shoots Sid Halley in the stomach as the novel opens.

Andy (*Bonecrack*). Stable lad at Rowley Lodge stables.

Angelica (*The Edge*). The murder victim in the mystery play being performed on the race train.

Angus (*The Edge*). The head chef on the race train.

Anna (*Trial Run*). Colleague of Natasha, and dedicated Russian employee of the tourist service who does her best to see that Randall Drew enjoys his visit to Moscow.

Arknold, Greville (*Smokescreen*). The surly trainer of Nerissa Cavesey's horses in South Africa.

Arkwright, Mr. (*Blood Sport*). Neighbor of Gene Hawkins's father in Yorkshire from the time when Hawkins Sr. was a trainer. He provides a key piece of information that will allow Gene to identify the missing Chrysalis, when and if he is found. Apparently, Chrysalis likes sardines, a most unusual trait in a racehorse.

Arkwright, Vernon ("Haig's Death," *Field of Thirteen*). Jockey and rider of Fable, who is all set to change the fortunes of the brothers Arkwright in the upcoming Cloister Handicap Hurdle.

Arkwright, Villiers ("Haig's Death," *Field of Thirteen*). Trainer of Fable, and brother of the jockey Vernon Arkwright.

Arletti, Russell (*Bonecrack*). Neil Griffon's employer, who is not too happy that Neil is taking so long to sort out his father's affairs.

Armadale, Ken (*Whip Hand*). A research vet from the Equine Research Establishment in Newmarket. He does the postmortem on Gleaner and finds something very unusual.

Ashe, Nicholas (*Whip Hand*). Erstwhile boyfriend of Jenny, Sid Halley's ex-wife. Nicky has disappeared after involving her in a confidence trick that raised money for a nonexistent charity. Admiral Roland asks Sid to track Nicky down so he can be prosecuted and Jenny won't have to go to prison.

Axminster, James (*Nerve*). A prestigious trainer who gives Rob Finn rides on winning horses and helps him trap the villain.

Balterzersen, Lars (*Slay-Ride*). Chairman of the Norwegian Jockey Club.

Barbo, Minty and Warren (*High Stakes*). They are Alexandra Ward's cousins in Miami. Steven Scott visits her while she's staying with them, and he enlists their aid in starting his plan for revenge.

Barnes, Chico (*Odds Against; Whip Hand*). Sid Halley's friend and fellow investigator at the Hunt Radnor agency. In *Whip Hand*, Chico and Sid are a team of investigators: ". . . as a working companion I found him great: funny, inventive, persistent, and deceptively strong."

Barnet, Ricky (*Banker*). A troubled teenager who tries to murder Calder Jackson.

Barnette, Major (*Bonecrack*). Racehorse owner who is skeptical of Neil Griffon's abilities to run his father's stables properly.

Barty (*Smokescreen*). Greville Arnold's head lad, who seems to terrify all of the stable lads that he supervises.

Barzini, Gabriella (*Flying Finish*). She works in the gift shop at the Milan airport. Henry Grey falls in love with her at first sight, and his love for her helps to change his life and outlook radically.

Baudelaire, Bill (*The Edge*). Head of security for the Canadian Jockey Club.

Baudelaire, Mrs. (*The Edge*). Bill Baudelaire's mother. She takes messages very competently for Tor Kelsey, in spite of being terminally ill. Tor becomes very fond of her in spite of their never having met in person.

Baxter, Lloyd (*Shattered*). The owner of Tallahassee, the horse that Martin Stukely is riding when he dies in a fall. He is a "grumpy, dumpy millionaire" who is mysteriously unconscious in Gerard Logan's shop on New Year's Eve 1999 while somebody is stealing the crucial videotape.

Bayst, Kenny (*Rat Race*). A jockey who gets assaulted by hired thugs when he refuses to lose races to order.

Beach, Tony (*Proof*). The hero. He is a wine merchant who is in mourning for his wife Emma. She has died in childbirth six months before the novel opens. He misses her deeply, and is lonely and depressed. He has a nose for telling one wine or whisky from another simply by smelling and tasting them. His talent becomes very useful when a local restaurateur appears to be passing off cheap wine and Scotch as expensive brands.

Beckett, Colonel (*For Kicks*). Steward of the National Hunt Committee, who along with his co-stewards employs Daniel Roke as an undercover investigator. Slender, ill-looking, with a weak clasp when he shakes hands. Eventually he has an interesting and life-changing proposition for Daniel Roke.

Bell, Jiminy (*Knockdown*). Once a steeplechase jockey, he has fallen on hard times and spends much of his time imbibing in racecourse bars.

Bellamy, Mr. ("Raid at Kingdom Hill," *Field of Thirteen*). Member of the Executive Committee at Kingdom Hill Racecourse who thinks security is the prime priority.

Bellbrook, Arthur (*Hot Money*). Elderly gardener who works for Malcolm Pembroke at his home, Quantum.

Benchmark, Patsy (*To the Hilt*). The daughter of Sir Ivan Westering. She is very protective of the inheritance that she expects to get from her father, and worried that Alexander Kinloch will interfere with that legacy.

Benchmark, Surtees (*To the Hilt*). Patsy's husband, and Alexander's declared enemy. He has a vicious streak that Patsy doesn't see at all.

Bergen, Clare (*Reflex*). Dynamic daughter of Samantha who is a fledgling director in a publishing company. Her interest in Philip Nore's photographs enables Philip to see that he has an alternative to being a jockey.

Bergen, Samantha (*Reflex*). One of the friends of the late Caroline Nore, with whom Philip lived for a while as a child. In tracing his roots, Philip rediscovers Samantha and meets her daughter Clare.

Berit (*Slay-Ride*). An elderly woman who was once nurse to young Mikkel Sandvik.

Bert (*Dead Cert*). Thug; part of a group who delivers a nasty message to Alan York to mind his own business.

Bert (*For Kicks*). Smelly, bed-wetting, deaf lad in the stables of Hedley Humber.

Bethune, Isobel (*10 Lb. Penalty*). Long-suffering wife of would-be politician Paul Bethune.

Bethune, Paul (*10 Lb. Penalty*). George Juliard's opponent in his race for a seat in Parliament. A businessman who is a vocal proponent of family values, he has been caught cheating on his wife.

Bill ("Corkscrew," *Field of Thirteen*). Security guard, receptionist, and factotum at the condominium development where Sandy Nutbridge lives.

Billington Innes, Jasper ("Haig's Death," *Field of Thirteen*). Bankrupt businessman, he thinks his horse Lilyglit is the only way out of his current financial mess.

Billington Innes, Wendy ("Haig's Death," *Field of Thirteen*). Wife to Jasper, she finds her perfect life crumbling around her.

Binsham, the Hon. Mrs. Marjorie (*Decider*). Lord Stratton's sister, and the matriarch of the decidedly odd Stratton family. "Marjorie will do anything to keep family affairs private," according to Dart Stratton.

Bob (*Trial Run*). Gardener and right-hand man of HRH the Prince.

Bognor, Bimmo (*For Kicks*). Bookie.

Boles, Piper ("The Gift," *Field of Thirteen*). A jockey nearing the end of his career, he's willing to make money about any way he can, including fixing a swindle at the Kentucky Derby.

Bolingbroke, Oliver ("Song for Mona," *Field of Thirteen*). Olympic gold medalist and husband of American country singer Cassidy Lovelace Ward, he gives Mona Watkins a job and the kind of home she's dreamed of having.

Bolt, Ellis (*Odds Against*). A crooked stockbroker, and Zanna Martin's boss.

Bone, Calvin (*Dead Cert*). Racecourse valet at Maidenhead where the novel opens.

Boston, Charlie (*Forfeit*). Owner of a string of betting shops, he started doing business the ordinary way. Then he expanded and turned into a bully, using two ex-boxers to collect from customers who are slow to pay.

Bracken, Betty (*Come to Grief*). She owns a colt whose hoof has been cut off, and calls Sid about it. She is also the long-suffering aunt of a sulky teenager, Jonathan.

Brad (*Straight*). An unemployed welder from Ipswich, he earns extra money acting as chauffeur and bodyguard to Derek Franklin. Though a man of few words, he saves Derek's bacon in more ways than one.

Bredon, John (*Bonecrack*). Trainer who is supposed to be taking over at Rowley Lodge stables while the elder Griffon is in hospital. Because of the tense situation involving young Rivera, Neil Griffon puts him off and runs the stables himself.

Brevett, Constantine (*Knockdown*). A wealthy businessman and a regular on the racecourse scene, he is engaged to the wealthy American, Mrs. Kerry Sanders. He is also the father of the edgy young steeplechase jockey, Nicol Brevett.

Brevett, Nicol (*Knockdown*). Temperamental young steeplechase jockey, he is the son of wealthy Constantine Brevett, fiancé of Mrs. Kerry Sanders.

Brickell, Angela (*Longshot*). She is a stable lad who has disappeared after getting in trouble for allegedly doping a racehorse.

Bricknell, Mavis and Walter (*The Edge*). Racehorse owners who are characters in the mystery play staged on the race train.

Briggs, Victor (*Reflex*). Owner of a number of horses that Philip Nore rides. A hard-nosed businessman with some shady connections, he sometimes asks Philip to lose races deliberately.

Britt, Miss (*Blood Sport*). Newspaper employee in Lexington who assists Gene Hawkins in compiling some very helpful information.

Britten, Roland (*Risk*). The hero. An amateur jockey and an accountant by profession, he wakes up one day to find himself completely in the dark, tied up, with only the sound of an engine close by. He has no idea where he is, why he is there, or how he will get himself out of the situation. But methodically he works through the problem and discovers the truth behind this kidnapping and other attempts on his life.

Brothersmith, Mr. (*Whip Hand*). George Caspar's veterinarian.

Brown, Leslie (*The Edge*). She is in charge of the horse car on the race train; Tor Kelsey thinks of her as the dragon that guards the treasure.

Budley, Bobby (*Risk*). A jockey who breaks his leg in a race, he has been a client of Roland Britten's. Roland's nemesis makes use of their connection for his own ends.

Bunt, Beatrice de Brescou (*Bolt*). Sister of Roland de Brescou, she wreaks havoc in the de Brescou household by siding with the violent Henri Nanterre.

Burley, George (*The Edge*). The conductor of the racing train.

Canterfield, Charlie (*High Stakes*). A wealthy merchant banker who becomes a close friend and ally of Steven Scott.

Carlo (*Bonecrack*). A vicious minder, employed by Enso Rivera, whose job it is to see that Rivera's instructions are carried out.

Carteret (*Decider*). An old chum of Lee Morris from architecture school. His old collection of diaries helps Lee find out more about Wilson Yarrow.

Carthy-Todd, Charles (*Rat Race*). An insurance man.

Caspar, George (*Whip Hand*). A racehorse trainer, married to the loud and angry Rosemary. The best horses in his stables have been losing lately, and nobody has been able to find out why.

Caspar, Rosemary (*Whip Hand*). The wife of prominent and successful trainer George Caspar, she is a "tough lady." She asks Sid Halley to help her ensure that their horse Tri-Nitro, a heavy favorite, isn't interfered with before a big race. Two of their horses have lost races unexpectedly, and she suspects trouble.

Cass (*For Kicks*). Head lad in the stables of Hedley Humber.

Cassavetes, Jik (*In the Frame*). An old friend of Charles Todd from art school. Jik has moved to Australia and married Sarah. Charles says of him: "Jik Cassavetes, long-time friend, my opposite in almost everything . . . Bearded, which I was not. Exuberant, noisy, extravagant, unpredictable; qualities I envied. Blue eyes and sun-blond hair. Muscles that left mine gasping. An outrageous way with girls. An abrasive tongue; and a wholehearted contempt for the things I painted." Jik and Sarah are with Charles all the way on his Australian investigation.

Cassavetes, Sarah (*In the Frame*). Recently married to Jik, she is not thrilled when Charles Todd's arrival in Australia interrupts their honeymoon. At first she is apprehensive that Jik will be injured, but eventually she becomes just as enthusiastic a participant in the chase as are Charles and Jik.

Cathcart, India (*Come to Grief*). She is a columnist on the dodgy tabloid newspaper *The Pump*. Her column includes some of the most savage attacks on Sid Halley's integrity.

Catto, Valentine (*The Edge*). Head of the Security Services for the British Jockey Club.

Cavesey, Danilo (*Smokescreen*). The nephew and heir of Link's friend Nerissa Cavesey. He is a student at the University of California Berkeley, and is described as a classic California golden boy.

Cavesey, Nerissa (*Smokescreen*). An old friend of Link's who asks him to check on the welfare of her horses in South Africa. Nerissa is dying of cancer, and Link feels that he must follow her wishes.

Cawdor-Jones, Major Kevin ("Raid at Kingdom Hill," *Field of Thirteen*).

Manager of Kingdom Hill Racecourse who has to confront his worst nightmare when a bomb threat is made against the course.

Cecil (*For Kicks*). Alcoholic lad in the stables of Hedley Humber.

Cenci, Alessia (*The Danger*). The kidnapped daughter of a rich Italian businessman. Andrew Douglas gets her back home safely, and helps her recover emotionally afterward. She had been one of the best women jockeys in Europe before her ordeal.

Cenci, Ilaria (*The Danger*). Alessia's jealous sister.

Cenci, Paolo (*The Danger*). Alessia Cenci's father. He pays a huge ransom to get her back from kidnappers.

Chand, Dr. Ravi (*Second Wind*). The physician who diagnoses and cures Perry Stuart's mystery illness. He is ecstatic about discovering a new disease, and asks Perry for permission to use him as a human guinea pig in order to further his research.

Chanter (*Rat Race*). A hippie art teacher and old art school friend of Nancy Ross. He keeps turning up at races and bothering her. "She couldn't decide whether he was Chanter the amorous buffoon or Chanter the frustrated sex maniac. Nor could I. I understood her needing help when he was around."

Charlie (*For Kicks*). Ex-con and lad in the stables of Hedley Humber.

Charter, Kenneth (*Proof*). Owner of a transport company whose lorry loads of whisky are being systematically stolen.

Checkov, Bert (*Forfeit*). An elderly racing correspondent with a drinking problem, he admonishes Ty Tyrone not to "sell his column." Not long afterward, he dies in a strange accident. Ty subsequently discovers that Checkov had been touting in his column horses who couldn't fail to win, but who somehow failed to show up on race day.

Chester, John ("Haig's Death," *Field of Thirteen*). Trainer for whom Moggie Reilly rides.

Christopher, Mr. (*Reflex*). Young employee of a firm specializing in photographic printing paper. Though not much help in answering Philip Nore's questions, he does find the one employee of the firm who can.

Chulitsky, Yuri Ivanovich (*Trail Run*). Russian architect who proves instrumental in connecting Randall Drew with important sources during his investigation in Moscow.

Cibber (*Wild Horses*). A character in the movie Thomas Lyon is filming. Thomas finds it easier to refer to the actor portraying the role by his character name. Cibber is based on the late Rupert Visborough.

Clark, Derry (*Forfeit*). A fellow reporter of Ty Tyrone's at the *Sunday Blaze*. He writes the calm and ordinary stuff, while Ty goes after the juicier, more controversial stories.

Clark, Valentine (*Wild Horses*). Once upon a time a blacksmith, he later became a highly successful racing journalist. He and Thomas Lyon have been friends since Thomas was a young boy and Valentine shod the horses in Thomas's grandfather's racing stables. On his deathbed he mutters what seems to be a confession of murder and involves Thomas in a very tricky situation.

Clem (*Dead Cert*). Racecourse valet at Maidenhead where the novel opens.

Cleveland, David (*Slay-Ride*). The hero. At thirty-three, he seems young to be the chief investigator for Britain's Jockey Club, but he proves more than equal to the task of discovering what became of a missing British jockey and the puzzle behind why he vanished in the first place.

Clive, Matt (*Blood Sport*). One half of the duo who runs a guest ranch, the High Zee, in Wyoming, where Gene Hawkins gets an important lead in his search for the missing racehorse. Brother of Yola and not a man to be crossed lightly.

Clive, Yola (*Blood Sport*). One half of the duo who runs a guest ranch, the High Zee, in Wyoming, where Gene Hawkins gets an important lead in his search for the missing racehorse. Sister to Matt.

Cloony, Peter (*Nerve*). A jockey whose livelihood is destroyed by persistent rumors of lateness and unreliability. Rob Finn stays overnight once with him and his pregnant wife; they have very little money and a very small and bare house.

Coconut (*Longshot*). Nearly fifteen and nicknamed for his abundant head of hair, Coconut is Gareth Vickers's best friend. John Kendall shows Gareth and Coconut some survival techniques in their local woodlands, and they are fascinated.

Collyer, Fred ("The Gift," *Field of Thirteen*). A once talented journalist, now almost down-and-out thanks to his alcohol intake, he's about to get a chance to redeem himself with a brewing big story at the Kentucky Derby. If only he can make use of the gift of a story.

Compass, Greg (*Wild Horses*). A former championship jockey now turned television personality, he assists Thomas Lyon by giving him a chance to go on the air with Nash Rourke and refute the rumors of dissent between director and star on the movie set.

Conrad (*Smokescreen*). A talented and Oscar-winning director of photography who has worked on Link's most recent film. He and Evan Pentelow go with Link to Kruger Park.

Cook, Thomas (*Dead Cert*). Course attendant at Maidenhead racecourse at the position closest to the site of Bill Davidson's accident. He disappears shortly after the accident.

Corunna, Carl ("Corkscrew," *Field of Thirteen*). A lawyer and a colleague of Patrick Green's.

Cox, Emily Jane (*To the Hilt*). Alexander Kinloch's estranged wife. She is a racehorse trainer with her own stables in Lambourn. Alexander and Emily have lived separately for some time, but they still like each other; they simply can't live together and do their work effectively.

Craig, Etty, aka Henrietta (*Bonecrack*). Head stable hand at Rowley Lodge stables, one of a few women in such an important position.

Cranfield, Dexter (*Enquiry*). A snobbish but hardworking trainer whose license is lifted unjustly; Kelly Hughes works for him. The father of Roberta Cranfield, who seems to have inherited his snobbery. Roberta fears he might kill himself when he loses his license; Kelly visits him and encourages him to hope that they might get their livelihoods back again.

Cranfield, Roberta (*Enquiry*). Daughter of Dexter Cranfield, the trainer for whom Kelly Hughes regularly rides. She asks Hughes for help, and they become friends. He thinks she's snobbish at first, but they work together to clear the charges against her father and Hughes.

Cratchet, Paul (*Shattered*). "Pernickety Paul" is Police Constable Catherine Dodd's partner, and he has watched over her like a father.

Cressie, Harbourn ("The Gift," *Field of Thirteen*). Trainer of Pincer Movement, one of the hopefuls for the Kentucky Derby.

Crest, Denby (*Risk*). A solicitor, he is a special client of Trevor King's. Roland Britten runs afoul of him while trying to do his job.

Crispin, Chief Superintendent ("The Day of the Losers," *Field of Thirteen*). The policeman who acts upon knowledge that banknotes from a robbery have been passed at the Grand National at Aintree.

Croft, Freddie (*Driving Force*). The hero. Freddie is a retired jockey who runs his own horse transport business.

Croft, Lizzie (*Driving Force*). Freddie's older sister, who is a physics professor at Edinburgh University. She pilots her own helicopter and comes to Freddie's aid when he needs her expertise.

Cross, Mrs. (*Odds Against; Whip Hand*). Admiral Roland's housekeeper at Aynsford.

Crossmead, Rufus (*10 Lb. Penalty*). Editor of *SHOUT!*, a scandal rag that publishes scurrilous rumors about Ben Juliard.

Curtiss, Robin (*Bolt*). Young veterinarian who tends to the horses of the

Princess Casilia de Brescou. He tells Kit Fielding about the so-called humane killer, the "bolt," which is used to kill several of the princess's horses.

Curzon, Ronnie (*Longshot*). John Kendall's literary agent, who gets him the job of writing Tremayne Vickers's biography.

Dace, J. L. (*Dead Cert*). Clerk of the course of Maidenhead racecourse.

Dainsee (*Bonecrack*). Young veterinarian who attends to the horses at Rowley Lodge stables.

d'Alban, Jimmy (*Proof*). Secretary to trainer Jack Hawthorn. He tells Tony Beach about some switched liquor at the Silver Moondance Restaurant.

Darcy, Evelyn (*Second Wind*). She is married to Robin, and seems much tougher and more unpleasant than he is.

Darcy, Madeleine (*Bolt*). The English wife of a French horse trainer, she has nothing good to say about Henri Nanterre.

Darcy, Robin (*Second Wind*). Robin lives in Florida, and farms turf and mushrooms. He encourages Kris Ironside in his desire to fly through the eye of a hurricane. He even buys a small plane in which Kris can achieve his dream—as long as he stops off at a deserted Caribbean island to do an errand for Robin.

Darwin, John (*Comeback*). Peter Darwin's adoptive father, a career diplomat in the Foreign Service.

Darwin, Margaret Perry (*Comeback*). Peter Darwin's mother; she provides her son with some key information about an old tragedy that occurred when she and Peter lived in the Cheltenham area, before she married John Darwin.

Darwin, Peter, aka Peter Perry (*Comeback*). The hero. A career diplomat in the Foreign Service, Darwin is on his way home for a vacation and a new posting in England when he becomes entangled in the lives of acquaintances who will need his skills in getting out of a dangerous situation. Darwin's mother had married a diplomat, John Darwin, who adopted Peter as his own son when Peter was twelve, and thus Peter grew up in the diplomatic lifestyle, as his family were posted around the world in the Foreign Service.

Davidson, Major Bill (*Dead Cert*). An amateur steeplechase jockey who dies after taking a fall from his horse, Admiral, at the beginning of the story.

Davidson, Scilla (*Dead Cert*). Wife and then widow of Major Bill Davidson; mother to their three children, Henry (eight), William (five), and Polly (the eldest). Henry's penchant for listening to phone conversations when he shouldn't provides an important clue for the solution of the mystery.

Davis, Ronald and Sue (*Forfeit*). Couple who are neighbors of Ty Tyrone and his wife, Elizabeth. They can often be counted on to help with Elizabeth when Ty needs a little bit of extra assistance.

Dawkins, Mrs. Robin ("Collision Course," *Field of Thirteen*). One of the three owners of a newspaper conglomerate, she is worried about the bottom line and looking for a new editor to work miracles.

Dawson (*Bolt*). Butler to the de Brescous.

Deansgate, Trevor (*Whip Hand*). An up-and-coming bookie, he owns the Billy Bones bookmaking business. Originally, his name was Trevor Shummuck; he has a brother, Barry Shummuck.

Debbie (*Risk*). One of the two long-suffering and rather inefficient assistants in the accountancy firm in Newmarket in which Roland Britten is the junior partner.

de Brescou, Casilia (*Bolt; Break In*). Owner of a number of champion racehorses, she is a princess of a dispossessed European monarchy and is married to an immensely wealthy but elderly and disabled French aristocrat.

de Brescou, Danielle (*Bolt; Break In*). Niece of Monsieur de Brescou and the Princess Casilia. She is American but is living in England and working as a television reporter. Kit Fielding falls in love with her on first sight.

de Brescou, Roland (*Bolt; Break In*). An elderly and immensely rich French aristocrat, he is the husband of the Princess Casilia. He must seek the aid of Kit Fielding in *Bolt*, when his family and his business interests are threatened by his erstwhile partner, Henri Nanterre.

Dee-Dee (*Longshot*). Secretary to Tremayne Vickers.

De Jong, Mike (*Forfeit*). Newsman who works on a paper that is the *Sunday Blaze*'s deadly rival. With a little urging, he provides Ty Tyrone with the scoop on the mysterious South African, Vjoersterod.

Dembley, Charles (*Forfeit*). Former owner of the racehorse Brevity. After being victimized by the scheme in which horses are removed from races at the last minute, he sold all his horses. He reluctantly gives Ty Tyrone some key information in his quest to find out who is behind the scheme.

den Relgan, Dana (*Reflex*). Beautiful young daughter of Ivor den Relgan, whose ability to bewitch an influential man helps her father gain the position in British racing circles he wants.

den Relgan, Ivor (*Reflex*). Brash, self-important man of dubious antecedents who has thrown about a lot of money, trying to inveigle his way into the upper echelons of British racing.

Dereham, Crispin (*Knockdown*). Elder brother (by one year) of Jonah Dereham, he has a drinking problem that renders him virtually unemployable. Filled with self-pity and self-loathing, he leeches a living off his brother, who puts up with him and does his best to look after him.

Dereham, Jonah (*Knockdown*). The hero. A former steeplechase jockey, he now makes a living as a bloodstock agent. He has a shoulder that becomes dislocated at the most inconvenient times, rendering him nearly helpless.

Derry, Jonathan (*Twice Shy*). The hero. A physics master and head of department at a public school, he finds himself in trouble when a friend, a computer programmer, gives him cassette tapes containing a program for handicapping horses. He is also a member of the British rifle team, having participated in the Olympics; his skill comes in handy when he has to outwit the villains at a key point. He is married to Sarah and is the older brother of William.

Derry, Meredith (*Wild Horses*). A retired professor of medieval history, late of Trinity College, he is an expert on the history of weaponry. He provides Thomas Lyon with some key information about the knives used in murderous attacks on various people.

Derry, Sarah (*Twice Shy*). The wife of Jonathan Derry, she has grown somewhat estranged from her husband, despondent over her inability to bear a child.

Derry, William (*Twice Shy*). The hero. The younger brother of Jonathan Derry, he has only one thing on his mind: horses. Though he eventually grew too big to fulfill his ambitions as a jockey, he makes a successful transition into a burgeoning career as a manager for racing magnate Luke Houston.

Dodd, Detective Constable Catherine (*Shattered*). She is sent to talk to Gerard Logan after his shop is robbed on New Year's Eve. She often works in plain clothes, along with her partner, Pernickety Paul. Gerard is immediately attracted to her, and the feeling is mutual.

Doone, Chief Inspector (*Longshot*). He leads the investigation into the murder of Angela Brickell.

Douglas, Andrew (*The Danger*). The hero. He works for Liberty Market, a firm that specializes in helping retrieve kidnap victims and in preventing kidnappings.

Drew, Randall (*Trial Run*). The hero. A highly successful amateur steeplechase jockey who has recently retired from racing to his farm in Warwickshire. He is no longer able to race due to his poor eyesight and the rules that preclude his wearing glasses while he races. Unable to wear contact lenses, he gives up racing to run his farm. He also has chronic respiratory problems, which make him prey to bronchial infections. Most of the time, however, he is able to control these problems with medication. Because of his aristocratic connections and his knowledge of the racing world, he is selected to carry out a sensitive mission in Russia involving the fate of a young British aristocrat who hopes to make the British Olympic team for the Moscow Games in 1980.

Driffield, Percy ("Haig's Death," *Field of Thirteen*). Leading trainer and father of Sarah, he's frustrated with Jasper Billington Innes's plan to sell Lilyglit.

Driffield, Sarah ("Haig's Death," *Field of Thirteen*). Daughter of a champion trainer, she's been sleeping with Moggie Reilly, who rides for her father's chief competitor.

Duke, Johnnie ("Nightmare," *Field of Thirteen*). Light-fingered hitch-hiker who aids Martin Retsov in his scheme to steal a horse, he turns out to have a secret of his own.

Durridge, Sir Vivian (*10 Lb. Penalty*). Wealthy trainer of racehorses. He dismissed Ben Juliard from his stables after receiving false information that Ben had been sniffing glue. Later on he makes restitution for this in an important way.

Dusty (*Bolt; Break In*). Head traveling lad for Wykeham Harlow.

Duveen, Pete (*High Stakes*). He drives a horse box and takes Steven Scott's racehorse Energise for a drive in the country one day. He plays an unwitting role in Steven's game of revenge.

Eaglewood, J. Rolls (*Comeback*). A racing notable in Cheltenham and the father of Russet Eaglewood of the shady reputation.

Eaglewood, Russet (*Comeback*). Peter Darwin remembers her from his youth in the Cheltenham area as a girl who is supposedly easy to persuade to drop her knickers. She is the daughter of racing notable J. Rolls Eaglewood, and mother of Izzy, who was briefly a girlfriend of Ken McClure's. Darwin discovers for himself the truth about those rumors featuring Russet Eaglewood.

Ed (*Wild Horses*). Thomas Lyon's assistant.

Ekaterin, Tim (*Banker*). The hero. Tim is a merchant banker in the Paul Ekaterin Merchant Bank. He helps Oliver Knowles finance the purchase of a champion racehorse for his breeding farm. When the foals are damaged and a murder occurs, Tim is galvanized into finding the killer.

Ellery-Penn, Kate (*Dead Cert*). Beautiful, flirtatious young owner of the racehorse Heavens Above, niece of George and Deb Penn. Alan York falls in love with her at first sight.

Elroy, Sticks (*Risk*). So named for the extreme thinness of his legs, he is one of Roland Britten's jockey clients.

Emil (*The Edge*). The headwaiter on the race train. He is happy to have Tor Kelsey's assistance in serving meals.

England, Martin (*Whip Hand*). A trainer who's an old friend of Sid Halley. He asks Sid to ride one of his best horses, the Derby hopeful Flotilla, on a "working gallop," and Sid regains some peace and happiness from the experience.

English, Marigold (*Driving Force*). A trainer who has newly arrived in Pixhill, and already is using Freddie Croft's transport vans.

Erskine, Jay (*Break In*). Reporter who runs afoul of Kit Fielding, along with his colleague, Owen Watts.

Evans, Pamela Jane (*Shattered*). An assistant and apprentice in the glass-blowing shop of Gerard Logan.

Everard, Lewis (*Longshot*). Nolan Everard's brother. He perjures himself in an attempt to have Nolan acquitted on a manslaughter charge, but the brothers are still jealous of each other. "Nolan has the looks and the dash, Lewis is a drunk with brains. Nolan has courage and is thick, Lewis is a physical disaster but when he's sober he's a whiz at making money. Nolan is a crack shot, Lewis misses every pheasant he aims at. Lewis would like to be the glamorous amateur jockey and Nolan would like to be upwardly disgustingly rich. Neither will ever manage it, but that doesn't stop the envy."

Everard, Nolan (*Longshot*). An ambitious and aggressive amateur jockey who often rides for Tremayne Vickers. He is charged with manslaughter in the death of his girlfriend Olympia. Nolan and Lewis are cousins of Fiona Goodhaven.

Faddy (*Bonecrack*). Stable lad at Rowley Lodge stables.

Fairchild-Smith, Mrs. (*High Stakes*). One of two elderly and poverty-stricken sisters who happily and very quietly take care of Steven Scott's horse Black Fire.

Farringford, Lord John (*Trial Run*). Known as Johnny, twenty-five-year-old Lord Farringford is a hopeful for the British equestrian team for the 1980 Moscow Olympics. His connection to a dead German rider, Hans Kramer, has somehow linked him to a strange conspiracy in Moscow that threatens not only his life but possibly diplomatic relations between Britain and the Soviet Union.

Farway, Dr. Bruce (*Driving Force*). The new local doctor in Pixhill, who is alienating almost everyone in the village with his patronizing attitude.

Faulds, Mrs. Perdita (*Decider*). A mysterious stockholder in the Stratton Park racecourse.

Faulds, Penelope (*Decider*). Perdita's daughter, she is eighteen and works in her mother's hairdressing salon. She is almost the double in looks of Lee Morris's wife Amanda.

Ferns, Linda (*Come to Grief*). Rachel's mother, whose life is miserable due to her daughter's illness. She calls in Sid Halley when Rachel's pony has its hoof cut off.

Ferns, Rachel (*Come to Grief*). A child who is very ill, perhaps dying, of leukemia. Rachel owned a pony, Silverboy, whose hoof was cut off. She and Sid Halley become good friends, sharing their infirmities and their courage.

Ferth, Lord (*Enquiry*). Kelly Hughes enlists his help, as a member of the original board of enquiry, to investigate who has framed him. He eventually has a change of heart.

Field, F. Harold ("Collision Course," *Field of Thirteen*). Co-owner of a newspaper conglomerate, along with Mrs. Robin Dawkins and Russell Maudsley.

Fielder, Mr. (*Dead Cert*). Manager of Marconicars, the Brighton taxi service that Alan York suspects is a front for something sinister.

Fielding, Christmas, aka Kit (*Bolt; Break In*). The hero. A highly successful steeplechase jockey, he has a twin sister named Holly, and at times they share a telepathic form of communication. His telepathic ability extends to the horses he rides. He rides chiefly for the Princess Casilia, Madame de Brescou.

Fielding, Mr. (*Bolt; Break In*). Grandfather of Kit and Holly, he reared the children after they were orphaned at the age of two. He is estranged from Holly because of her marriage to Bobby Allardeck.

Filmer, Julius Apollo (*The Edge*). A racehorse owner, accused of murdering a stable lad who knew too much about Filmer's villainous schemes. He is on the Canadian race train. Tor Kelsey is sent along on the train to be sure Filmer doesn't do more harm.

Finch, Desmond (*To the Hilt*). The second-in-command, after Sir Ivan Westering, at the King Alfred Brewery.

Finch, Jossie (*Risk*). Attractive young woman, she catches Roland Britten's eye when she strolls into his firm on an errand for her father. Daddy is William Finch, master of Axwood Stables.

Finch, William (*Risk*). Master of Axwood Stables and father of the nubile Jossie, he is none too appreciative of Roland Britten's interest in his daughter nor of his skills as an accountant.

Finland, Jamie ("Blind Chance," *Field of Thirteen*). Fifteen years old and blind, he listens to the races on radio and TV, and one day he stumbles across a very interesting—and lucrative—fiddle at Ascot.

Finn, Joanna (*Nerve*). She is Rob Finn's first cousin. She knows that Rob loves her, but she doesn't want to get involved romantically with him as the bloodlines are too close. She is a singer, a classical musician, like the rest of his family.

Finn, Rob (*Nerve*). The hero. Rob is a steeplechase jockey whose mounts begin to lose just as he's making a success of himself. People say he's lost his nerve. He knows that he has not.

Finnegan, Dermot (*Forfeit*). An undistinguished jockey with a comparable mount in the Lamplighter Gold Cup whom Ty Tyrone interviews for his article on the race.

Fitzwalter, Fitz (*Comeback*). A scrap metal merchant who is also a racehorse owner. Though one of his horses died while under Ken McClure's care, he remains willing to believe in Ken's innocence of malpractice.

Floyd, Yvonne (*Comeback*). One of the two small-animal vets associated with Carey Hewett's veterinary practice in Cheltenham.

Flynn, David, aka Zak (*The Edge*). The leading actor as well as the writer of the mystery play performed on the transcontinental race train.

Folk, Jeremy (*Reflex*). Young solicitor charged with getting Philip Nore to comply with the wishes of Philip's unpleasant, autocratic grandmother before she dies.

Force, Dr. Adam (*Shattered*). Also known to Gerard Logan as "whitebeard." He lives in Devon, and seems to be doing good work at a local nursing home.

Ford, Amy (*Second Wind*). She and her husband Michael live in luxury on Grand Cayman Island. They sell their small plane to Robin Darcy so that Kris Ironside can fly it into Hurricane Odin. Amy is very rich and comes from the "grand-house-in-the-country" level of English society.

Ford, Michael (*Second Wind*). Amy's husband, he is "a shade lower in the social hierarchy" than his wife, "however bulging the coffers." He has made his millions from owning a chain of gyms. "Scarcely taller than Robin Darcy, Michael Ford, with his tanned bare broad-shouldered torso and his strong shoe-and-sockless slightly bowed brown legs, looked like the useful muscle that the rounded Robin lacked."

Fordham, Foster (*10 Lb. Penalty*). An expert on the sabotaging of race cars, he consults with George Juliard over the tampering incident with Juliard's Range Rover.

Fox, Norton (*Forfeit*). Trainer of Zig Zag, a favorite for the Lamplighter Gold Cup. Ty Tyrone interviews him while he's tracking down whoever is behind the scheme that brought Bert Checkov to his death.

Franklin, Derek (*Straight*). The hero. A successful steeplechase jockey, at thirty-four he is at the height of his career when he is sidelined by an injury. His elder brother Greville's sudden death in a horrible accident lands him in a tricky situation; he has to take over Greville's gemstone import business without knowing the least thing about it, or indeed, much about his brother's life. The more he delves into his brother's secrets, however, the deeper he finds himself in a dangerous situation. He must learn to think like his brother in order to decipher Greville's secrets, thereby saving Greville's business and his own life.

Franklin, Greville (*Straight*). Horribly injured in an accident, he dies, leaving his gemstone import business, Saxony Franklin, in the capable hands of his younger brother. With a penchant for gadgets of all kinds, a love of secrecy, and an innate streak of honesty, he unwittingly made himself the target for several unscrupulous men.

Frazer, Samson (*10 Lb. Penalty*). Editor of *The Hoopwestern Gazette*, he has to rein in his rogue reporter, Usher Rudd.

Frederick, Johnny (*Risk*). A friend of Roland Britten since their schoolboy days, he is the owner of a shipwright business. He is able to assist Roland in tracking down the vessel upon which he was held captive and the man who captained the boat.

Freemantle, Morgan (*The Danger*). A Jockey Club official who is kidnapped while on a visit to a racecourse near Washington, D.C.

Friarly, Lord Philip (*Whip Hand*). He owns racehorses. Sid Halley used to ride for him, and now he asks Sid to look into why some horses that are owned by syndicates are not doing as well as expected. Lord Friarly is an "earl, landowner, and frightfully decent fellow . . . He was of the old school of aristocrats: sixtyish, beautifully mannered, genuinely compassionate, slightly eccentric, and more intelligent than people expected."

Frisby, Bananas, aka John James (*Twice Shy*). A longtime friend of William

Derry's, he keeps a pub in the village near where William lives. He proves to be a staunch ally when William is attacked by Angelo Gilbert.

Frost, Detective Inspector (*In the Frame*). He is in charge of the investigation into Regina Stuart's murder. Charles Todd feeds him information about what he finds out in Australia, and Frost gives him some help in return, but generally he's not terribly helpful or compassionate.

Gardner, Brett (*Driving Force*). A horse van driver who breaks Freddie Croft's company rules one night and picks up a hitchhiker, only to have the mystery man die in his van. Freddie is thinking of firing Brett anyway, as he is an incorrigible whiner and complainer who "sow[s] his own dissatisfaction like a virus."

Gardner, Mrs. (*Decider*). Roger's wife, who helps take care of the Morris boys, and feeds them plenty of fruitcake.

Gardner, Roger (*Decider*). Manager of Stratton Park racecourse. He asks Lee Morris for his help in keeping the racecourse going.

George (*Bonecrack*). Stable lad at Rowley Lodge stables.

George (*Wild Horses*). The character portrayed by Nash Rourke in the movie and based on Jackson Wells, the trainer whose young wife was found hanged in the stables.

Ghost (*Second Wind*). The British government agent John Rupert calls "Ghost" in as another expert to help Perry Stuart in his investigation.

Gibbons, Major Colly (*Forfeit*). Despite the fact that his wife has just decamped with an American colonel, he provides Ty Tyrone with information on his handicapping of the Lamplighter Gold Cup. He is much in demand for his skills at handicapping.

Gideon, Ezra (*The Edge*). An aristocratic owner of a promising two-year-old racehorse. It's a surprise to all when he sells the horse to Julius Filmer and shortly thereafter commits suicide.

Gilbert, Angelo (*Twice Shy*). The violent son of businessman Harry Gilbert, he tries, not always successfully, to bully Jonathan and William Derry into getting what he wants.

Gilbert, Harry (*Twice Shy*). The owner of a successful bingo empire and a string of betting shops, he is interested in buying Liam O'Rorke's handicapping system. He is the father of the volatile Angelo, whose penchant for violence causes great trouble for both Jonathan and William Derry.

Giles (*The Edge*). The murderer in the mystery play being performed on the race train.

Gill, Robbie (*Wild Horses*). Young doctor who sees after Dorothea Pannier and Valentine Clark. He assists Tom Lyon in various ways.

Gillie (*Bonecrack*). Independent-minded heiress, thirty-six, who is Neil Griffon's tenant in his house in London. She is also his lover, an unconventional woman who has no interest in marriage.

Ginge (*Bonecrack*). Stable lad at Rowley Lodge stables.

Glenn, Austin Dartmouth ("The Day of the Losers," *Field of Thirteen*). With a thick wad of banknotes in his possession, which he was supposed to sit on for five years, he heads out for the Grand National at Aintree. How much trouble can he possibly find for himself?

Glitberg (*Risk*). With his partner Ownslow, he ran a construction racket that bilked the unwary of untold millions, until he was bested by Roland Britten.

Goldenberg, Eric (*Rat Race*). A passenger on Matt Shore's first, ill-fated plane trip to Haydock races. The large and angry Goldenberg seems to order jockey Kenny Bayst to lose races.

Goldoni, Bruno and Beatrice (*The Danger*). They own Brunelleschi, the great Italian horse that Alessia Cenci rides.

Goodhaven, Fiona (*Longshot*). She is Harry Goodhaven's wife. She owns the racehorse Chickweed, which was allegedly doped by Angela Brickell. Angela was later found murdered, and suspicion falls on Harry Goodhaven. Nolan and Lewis Everard are her cousins.

Goodhaven, Harry (*Longshot*). A wealthy and socially prominent race-horse owner. His horses are trained by Tremayne Vickers, and they live in the same village.

Gowery, Lord (*Enquiry*). The head of the board of enquiry that suspends Kelly Hughes. He may have some skeletons in his closet.

Grantchester, Oliver (*To the Hilt*). Sir Ivan Westering's lawyer. He disapproves of Alexander Kinloch.

Graves, Jasper (*Break In*). Nephew of the nasty Jermyn Graves.

Graves, Jermyn (*Break In*). Belligerent racehorse owner who tries to remove his horses from Bobby Allardeck's stables, until he is routed by Kit Fielding.

Green, Patrick ("Corkscrew," *Field of Thirteen*). A lawyer, he is seemingly a friend of Sandy Nutbridge, whom Sandy calls upon when he's arrested.

Greene, Mr. (*In the Frame*). A phony insurance investigator who raises the suspicions of Charles Todd.

Greenfield, Louis (*For Kicks*). A suspicious character who approaches Daniel Roke at a bar and sounds him out as a potential henchman in the doping scheme. Daniel first identifies him as "Black Moustache."

Greening, Gerald (*Bolt*). Solicitor to Roland de Brescou.

Gregory, Pete (*Dead Cert*). Burly racehorse trainer and former jockey in whose stables Admiral, Bill Davidson's horse, is trained.

Grey, Henry (*Flying Finish*). The hero. He works for an air transport firm that often flies horses to races in other countries. He is an aristocrat, and is properly called Lord Grey, but he doesn't have any money and doesn't like people to know about his family connections. His parents want him safely married and producing heirs, while he wants to fly planes and ride in steeplechases.

Griffon, Neil (*Bonecrack*). The hero. Self-described as a "thirty-four-year-old sober-minded businessman," Neil is attempting to bring order to his father's account books when he is viciously attacked by thugs. He grew up with an emotionally distant, critical father who is a racehorse trainer; he left when he finished school and started his own antiques business. He eventually sold that for a job, basically as an accountant, in which he sorts out companies in trouble. When his father is hospitalized for several weeks with a broken leg, following a car crash, Neil steps in to keep the stables running and finds himself in the midst of a tense situation.

Griffon, Neville (*Bonecrack*). Cantankerous owner of Rowley Lodge stables, father of Neil. Hospitalized with a broken leg after a car crash, he is resentful of his estranged son's success in running his training stables and does his best to undermine Neil.

Grits (*For Kicks*). Stable lad in the Earl of October's stables. Genial, but none too bright.

Gudrun (*Trial Run*). Amiable and attractive young West German exchange student who is a particularly close friend of the British student, Stephen Luce.

Guggenheim, Professor (*Driving Force*). A biology expert who helps Freddie Croft at an important time in the investigation.

Guirlande, Emil Jacques ("Dead on Red," *Field of Thirteen*). A professional assassin, afraid of flying, whose assignment is to kill one of England's beloved jockeys, Red Millbrook.

Guiseppe-Peter (*The Danger*). The mysterious kidnapper of Alessia Cenci and Dominic Nerrity. He plays opera music to his victims, and apparently has some connection to the racing world. He becomes Andrew Douglas's nemesis.

Haig, Christopher ("Haig's Death," *Field of Thirteen*). At forty-two, he's about to judge his last race, all unawares, at Winchester Spring Meeting, and his death will have interesting consequences for various players in the unfolding drama.

Halley, Jenny (*Odds Against*; *Whip Hand*). Sid's ex-wife. She gets into trouble in *Whip Hand* for using her name and money for a charity fund-raiser that turns out to be a confidence trick. When her father, Admiral Roland, enlists Sid Halley's assistance in helping Jenny avoid prosecution, she is fiercely resentful of her ex-husband's efforts.

Halley, Sid (*Odds Against*; *Whip Hand*; *Come to Grief*). Dick Francis's best-known series hero. Sid is a former champion steeplechase jockey whose hand was so badly injured in a racing accident that he had to give up riding. He becomes a private investigator with the Hunt Radnor Associates in *Odds Against*, but does little work for them until his father-in-law jolts him from his depression and dangles an interesting case in front of him. In later books he has his own agency and specializes in racing inquiries.

Harley, Crystal (*10 Lb. Penalty*). Mervyn Teck's secretary.

Harley, Honey (*Rat Race*). The air traffic controller and general factotum at the airport where Derrydown Sky Taxi service is headquartered.

Harlow, Jules Reginald ("Corkscrew," *Field of Thirteen*). A wealthy businessman with firm beliefs on justice, he finds that one act of philanthropy can have some quite unforeseen consequences.

Harlow, Mrs. ("Corkscrew," *Field of Thirteen*). The wife of businessman Jules Reginald Harlow.

Harlow, Wykeham (*Bolt; Break In*). Trainer of the horses belonging to the Princess Casilia de Brescou. Though his memory often fails him, he still has a magic touch in training champion racehorses.

Harris, Mr. (*Blood Sport*). Newspaper employee in Lexington who assists Gene Hawkins in compiling some very helpful information.

Hart, Angela ("Spring Fever," *Field of Thirteen*). Plump, motherly, and fifty-two, she falls in love with a twenty-four-year-old jockey and learns what the true cost of blind trust can be.

Harve (*Driving Force*). Freddie Croft's head driver.

Harvey, Belladonna, aka Bell (*Second Wind*). She and Kris Ironside have an on-again-off-again relationship, with frequent quarrels.

Harvey, Caspar (*Second Wind*). A crony of Kris Ironside, Caspar is a racehorse owner. He is friendly with Oliver Quigley and Robin Darcy.

Hawkins (*Dead Cert*). Subordinate of Inspector Lodge in the Maidenhead CID.

Hawkins, Gene (*Blood Sport*). The hero. An English intelligence agent, at thirty-eight he is battling life-threatening depression when his boss encourages him to search for millionaire Dave Teller's missing stallion. Worn down by his profession and by the loss of the woman he loves, Gene is due three weeks' leave when his boss, Simon Keeble, invites him on a boating outing, with an ulterior motive. Fearing that three weeks on his own might lead him to make an irrevocable choice, Gene agrees to the job of locating Teller's missing stallion, Chrysalis. Gene's father had been a trainer, and Gene has the necessary knowledge of horses to be suitable for this particular assignment. While doing the job, Gene encounters two women who pique his interest: Teller's alcoholic wife and Keeble's young, attractive daughter. He also makes a friend who ultimately helps change his life for the better.

Hawthorn, Flora (*Proof*). Wife of Jack Hawthorn. She asks Tony Beach to help them out in the aftermath of several deaths at their stables.

Hawthorn, Jack (*Proof*). A racehorse trainer. Multiple deaths occur in a dreadful accident at his stables, when a horse van rolls into a tent full of partygoers, including a wealthy sheik. He is a customer and friend of Tony Beach.

Hengelman, Sam (*Blood Sport*). Operates a private van service for moving horses out of Lexington, Kentucky. He assists Gene Hawkins in his covert moving of a racehorse from one location to another.

Henry (*Decider*). Henry is an old pal of Lee Morris, and is a "large-scale junk dealer." He rents circus tents to the Stratton Park racecourse after the stands are blown up by a bomb.

Herrick, Malcolm (*Trial Run*). British journalist, Moscow correspondent for *The Watch*, who belittles Randall Drew's chances of success in uncovering the identity of the mysterious Alyosha.

Hewett, Carey (*Comeback*). He is the senior partner in the veterinary practice where Ken McClure is one of the junior members. He seems devastated by the mishaps surrounding his once highly successful and well-respected practice, and some of his junior colleagues want to dump him and set up for themselves once disaster starts dogging them.

Hickory, John (*Shattered*). An assistant and apprentice in the glassblowing shop of Gerard Logan.

Higgins, Mr., aka Higgs (*Comeback*). An insurance agent for an agency that insures racehorses.

Higgs, Lenny (*The Edge*). The groom assigned to Daffodil Quentin's horse Laurentide Ice. He gets into trouble on the race train.

Highbury, George ("The Gift," *Field of Thirteen*). Trainer for Somerset Farms, he gives Piper Boles a hard time about his weight and his chances to ride Crinkle Cut in the Kentucky Derby.

Hillman, Dane (*Dead Cert*). Professional jockey and rising star in the steeplechase world; a rival of Alan York's for the affections of Kate Ellery-Penn.

Hitchins, Billy ("Blind Chance," *Field of Thirteen*). A young bookie, he sells Greg Simpson a fateful ticket at Ascot.

Hodge, Roderick (*Smokescreen*). A South African newspaper reporter.

Hodges, A. V., aka Mr. Smith (*Bolt*). A witness who helps tie Henri Nanterre to the scene of a potential crime.

Holth, Gunnar (*Slay-Ride*). Norwegian racehorse trainer; the missing jockey, Bob Sherman, had been staying with him before he disappeared.

Houston, Luke (*Twice Shy*). Owner of a highly successful bloodstock business, he hires William Derry to act as manager for his operation in England while his racing manager, Warrington Marsh, recuperates from a stroke.

Hoylake, Tommy (*Bonecrack*). The "second-best" jockey in Britain and among the dozen best in the world. He rides horses for Rowley Lodge stables, owned by Neil Griffon's father.

Huggerneck, Bert (*High Stakes*). A bookie's clerk who is an old friend of Charlie Canterfield. He helps Steven Scott and Charlie set a trap for the villains.

Hughes (*Dead Cert*). Member of Alan York's office staff in London.

Hughes, Kelly (*Enquiry*). The hero. He is framed, along with trainer Dexter Cranfield, for fixing a race. He launches his own enquiry in order to discover who framed them.

Hughes-Beckett, Rudolph (*Trial Run*). Highly placed official in the Foreign Office who recruits Randall Drew for the Moscow mission, despite his own antipathy toward the horse-racing crowd and his belief that the situation is not very serious.

Humber, Hedley (*For Kicks*). Stable owner and trainer who is notorious for his ill-treatment of stable lads, who seldom work at his stables for more than two or three months before moving on. Daniel Roke seeks employment in his stables in order to uncover the truth about the doping ring.

Huntercombe, Antonia (*Knockdown*). The aunt of Sophie Randolph, she is a racehorse owner and proprietor of Paley Stud. She gives Jonah Dereham some pertinent information about the pernicious side effects of the "kickback" policy that makes many bloodstock agents less than welcome with many owners who want to sell horses.

Hunterson, Harry (*Forfeit*). One of the "untypical" racehorse owners whom Ty Tyrone is interviewing for his article on the Lamplighter Gold Cup. He won his horse, Egocentric, in a raffle. He is married to Sarah, who looks somewhat askance at his mixed-race niece, Gail Pominga.

Hunterson, Sarah (*Forfeit*). Wife of Harry Hunterson and reluctant aunt-in-law to Gail Pominga.

Hurst, Hudson (*10 Lb. Penalty*). A politician whose star is definitely on the rise, he is George Juliard's chief rival as the fair-haired boy of the party and a leading contender to become the next prime minister.

Hutchings, Fred (*Comeback*). A colleague of Peter Darwin's, he is the British consul in Miami. He asks Darwin to help a British woman, Vicky Larch, and her husband, Greg Wayfield, after they have been violently attacked in Miami on the eve of their departure for England to attend Vicky's daughter's wedding.

Idris, Owen (*High Stakes*). Steven Scott's factotum, employed both in his house and his workshop. He helps Steven with his trap for the villain.

Ingersoll, Tick-Tock (*Nerve*). A fellow jockey and friend of Rob Finn's; they buy a car together and share its expenses. Tick-Tock is known for being a cheerful companion, at least until misfortune overtakes him.

Ingram, Eddy (*Knockdown*). A member of the "well-heeled unemployed," he is one of Jonah Dereham's best clients—until Jonah runs afoul of the group running a vicious kickback scheme.

Inskip (*For Kicks*). Trainer for the Earl of October's stables, and Daniel Roke's first boss in his undercover assignment.

Ireland, Bunty (*Bolt; Break In*). Racing reporter for the *Towncrier*.

Irestone, Detective Chief Superintendent (*Twice Shy*). The policeman in charge of the investigation of the murder of Chris Norwood.

Irish, John (*Shattered*). An assistant and apprentice in the glassblowing shop of Gerard Logan.

Ironside, Kris (*Second Wind*). Kris pilots his own small plane and, like his friend Perry Stuart, works as a meteorologist for BBC television. He is a manic-depressive and harbors frequent thoughts of suicide. Aside from his emotional swings, he is excellent company, and he and Perry often go for weekend trips in his Piper Cherokee. Unfortunately, he has a strong urge to fly through the eye of a hurricane, and he involves Perry in his ill-fated dream.

Isobel (*Driving Force*). One of Freddie Croft's secretaries.

Ivan (*Wild Horses*). A stuntman working on Thomas Lyon's movie.

Iverson, Vivian (*Risk*). A racing acquaintance of Roland Britten, he helps set up a meeting with the unsuspecting Roland and three of his nemeses.

Jackson, Calder (*Banker*). A healer who uses his own herbal mixtures and the laying on of hands to heal horses of many kinds of ills. Tim Ekaterin saves his life when a troubled teenager attempts to knife him.

Jardine, Jay (*Comeback*). The cattle specialist in Carey Hewett's veterinary practice in Cheltenham. He is one of the partners who seems eager to dump Hewett and Ken McClure and set up with some of the other junior members.

Jason (*Straight*). Muscular youth who handles the heavy work at Saxony Franklin; he doesn't seem to have much respect for Derek Franklin's abilities in filling his late brother's shoes.

Jenks, Prospero (*Straight*). A jeweler by profession, he is a friend and business associate of Greville Franklin's. He is anxious to get his hands on the diamonds that Greville had bought for him, for a commissioned piece.

Jerry (*For Kicks*). Mentally deficient lad in the stables of Hedley Humber. Daniel Roke befriends him during his tenure in the stables.

Jim (*Shattered*). A driver who is hired as bodyguard number three for Gerard Logan, after Worthington and Tom Pigeon.

Jimmy (*For Kicks*). Ex-con and lad in the stables of Hedley Humber.

Joan (*Dead Cert*). Nanny to the Davidson children.

Joe (*Break In*). Video editor who helps Kit Fielding put together a tape, which he uses to rein in Maynard Allardeck.

Jogger (*Driving Force*). The mechanic for Freddie Croft's horse transport firm. Jogger is a former army driver who served in Northern Ireland. He is killed in his inspection pit, after leaving Freddie a mysterious message.

John (*Dead Cert*). Journalist who provides Alan York with some important information.

John (*Banker*). A colleague of Tim Ekaterin's at the bank. He is constantly jealous and suspicious of Tim.

Johnston, Miss (*High Stakes*). One of two elderly and poverty-stricken sisters who run a small, dilapidated riding school and stables. They take care of Steven Scott's horse Black Fire.

Jonathan (*Come to Grief*). A sulky teenager and nephew of Betty Bracken. He is a much-needed helper for Sid Halley in his investigation, especially since Chico Barnes isn't working with Sid any longer.

Jones, Acey (*Rat Race*). A large, congenial Australian with a broken ankle and crutches. He is often to be found in racecourse bars, telling everyone within earshot how good his insurance payout was after an accident.

Jones, Frank (*Trial Run*). British schoolteacher on holiday in Russia whom Randall Drew meets at his hotel in Moscow. Frank's enthusiasm for the Russian way of life hides a deeper commitment, but he proves instrumental in saving Randall's life at one point in the story.

Jones, Priam (*Shattered*). The trainer whose horses Martin Stukely regularly rides.

Juliard, Benedict (*10 Lb. Penalty*). The hero. A few weeks shy of his eighteenth birthday, Ben Juliard is Francis's youngest hero. When he finds himself dismissed from the stables where he is training to become a jockey, Ben is taken immediately to see his father, George, who is about to mount a campaign for Parliament. Ben becomes his father's bodyguard and companion throughout the grueling election, protecting his father from someone who would rather see George Juliard dead than elected.

Juliard, George (*10 Lb. Penalty*). A wealthy young businessman, he has political ambitions. When he decides to run for parliament, he wants his only son, Benedict, by his side, since he has no other close family, his wife (and Ben's mother) having died at their son's birth.

June (*Straight*). Young employee at Saxony Franklin, she is a whiz at computers who enjoyed her employer's love of gadgetry. Her knowledge of Greville Franklin's habits and his gadgets proves to be invaluable in Derek's attempts to unlock his brother's many secrets.

Katya (*Smokescreen*). A reporter who is electrocuted by a microphone while talking to Edward Lincoln. The microphone had been intended for him to hold. Link saves her life by giving her CPR.

Keeble, Joan (*Blood Sport*). Wife of Gene Hawkins's boss.

Keeble, Lynnie, aka Linnet (*Blood Sport*). Daughter of Gene Hawkins's boss. Though he at first feels himself too old for her, Gene realizes that Lynnie could be the best thing for him, if he can wait long enough.

Keeble, Peter (*Blood Sport*). Young son of Gene Hawkins's boss, whose handiness with a camera provides Gene with an important clue to the plot surrounding Dave Teller.

Keeble, Simon (*Blood Sport*). Gene Hawkins's boss and friend who encourages him to take the job that American millionaire Dave Teller offers him.

Keene, Ziggy (*Wild Horses*). A stuntman whom Thomas Lyon calls upon for some extraordinary scenes he has in mind for his movie. He finds the wild Viking horses that Thomas wants for one very special scene.

Keith, Eddy (*Whip Hand*). The deputy director of the Jockey Club's Security Service. He is suspected of being corrupt.

Keithly, Donna (*Twice Shy*). Married to Peter, a computer programmer, she lands herself and her husband in big trouble by kidnapping someone else's child when she is despondent over her own inability to have children.

Keithly, Peter (*Twice Shy*). A computer programmer, he writes a program, based on Liam O'Rorke's notes, for handicapping horses. He is married to Donna, who causes great trouble for herself and her husband.

Kellar, Corin (*Nerve*). A trainer who is weak and nasty and only too willing to pass along unsavory rumors about jockeys. He is the trainer for whom Art Mathews, who shoots himself at the beginning of the book, has worked.

Kelsey, Tor (*The Edge*). The hero. He is an undercover investigator for the English Jockey Club. He is sent on a race train across Canada in order to foil the dastardly schemes of Julius Apollo Filmer.

Kemp-Lore, Maurice (*Nerve*). He is a journalist, with a very popular television show, *Turf Talk*. He comes from a family where everyone else is deeply involved with racing or showing horses, but unfortunately he has an asthma attack any time he gets near a horse. His approach to dealing with his family is contrasted with Rob Finn's similar situation.

Kendall, John (*Longshot*). The hero. He has written travel guides on how to survive in the jungle, the Arctic, and other remote places. He is now writing a novel, and needs a cheap place to live until it's finished. He agrees to write a biography of Tremayne Vickers, a famous racehorse trainer, and goes to live with him during the process.

Kennet, Trevor (*High Stakes*). A trainer in Newmarket. Steven Scott sends him his racehorses Wrecker, Hermes, and Bubbleglass.

Kenneth (*For Kicks*). Lad in the stables of Hedley Humber.

Kenny (*Reflex*). Stable lad in Harold Osborne's stables who used to work for Bart Underfield, at the time when five horses in Underfield's stables were shot to death.

Kiddo (*Blood Sport*). Stable lad at Orpheus Farm.

King, Trevor (*Risk*). Senior partner in the accountancy firm in which Roland Britten works. Big, expansive, he has allowed Roland time to pursue his amateur career along with his professional duties.

Kinloch, Alexander (*To the Hilt*). The hero. He is a painter who lives in the remote mountains of Scotland. He paints mostly pictures of golf courses and golfers, but also does portraits and other paintings. He paints the human spirit.

Kinloch, Earl of (*To the Hilt*). His name is Robert, but he is sometimes known to his family as Himself. He is Alexander's uncle and an old friend of Sir Ivan Westering.

Kinloch, James (*To the Hilt*). Alexander's cousin and heir to the earldom, he is a happy-go-lucky man with a sunny family life. James and Alexander love to play golf together.

Kinser, Dennis ("Collision Course," *Field of Thirteen*). An overly ambitious trainer who has plenty of schemes for getting ahead, until he runs afoul of Bill Williams.

Kinser, Pauline ("Collision Course," *Field of Thirteen*). Owner of the Mainstream Mile restaurant, and aunt of Dennis Kinser, where Bill Williams receives such shabby treatment that he retaliates in devastating fashion.

Kinship, Lance (*Reflex*). Film and television director with a reputation for gaining entry to elite circles by supplying drugs.

Kirk, Archie (*Come to Grief*). Betty Bracken's brother. He is a civil servant with a mysterious job and an appreciation of Sid Halley's talents as an investigator.

Kitchens, Mr. and Mrs. (*10 Lb. Penalty*). He is a local businessman who is a vocal supporter of Orinda Nagle, and this irritates his long-suffering wife to no end.

Kitchens, Sam (*Blood Sport*). Stable lad who looked after the missing stallion, Chrysalis. Gene Hawkins enlists his aid to identify the stallion.

Klugvoigt, Mr. (*Smokescreen*). The chairman of the Race Club at Germiston races in South Africa.

Knight, Marigold (*Shattered*). Rich and ditsy mother of Bon-Bon Stukely, she lends her talented chauffeur Worthington to Gerard Logan as a bodyguard.

Knowles, Ginnie (*Banker*). Daughter of Oliver Knowles, she is a talented, friendly, and bright teenager who leaves school to help out on her father's stud farm. She is enthusiastic and knowledgeable about horses, but not at all self-confident about herself. She becomes a firm friend of Tim Ekaterin.

Knowles, Oliver (*Banker*). The owner and operator of a stud farm. With the help of Tim Ekaterin and a very large loan from his bank, Oliver buys the champion racehorse Sandcastle for stud. He is the father of the charming teenager Ginnie Knowles.

Kraye, Doria (*Odds Against*). Married to Howard, and almost as evil and perverted as he is.

Kraye, Howard (*Odds Against*). A real estate investor and developer who wants to take over Seabury Racecourse in order to destroy it and build a housing estate. His wife, Doria, is nearly as vicious.

Kristiansen, Arne (*Slay-Ride*). Investigator for the Norwegian Jockey Club; also responsible for security at Ovrevoll racecourse in Oslo. Married to the beautiful Kari.

Kristiansen, Kari (*Slay-Ride*). An interior designer, she is married to Arne, who takes great pride in his beautiful and talented wife.

Lang, Zoe (*To the Hilt*). She is a retired professor and expert on antiquities. She believes passionately that important Scottish historical objects should belong to the state, not to individuals like the Earl of Kinloch.

Larch, Belinda (*Comeback*). A skilled veterinary nurse and the daughter of Vicky Larch, she is engaged to be married to talented veterinary surgeon Ken McClure. The prickly, jealous type, she is also inclined to be a bit ashamed of her more free-spirited and flirtatious mother.

Larch, Vicky (*Comeback*). A sixtyish professional singer who performs a nightclub act with her husband, Greg Wayfield. The night before she and her husband are to depart for England for her daughter's wedding, they are mugged, and Peter Darwin is enlisted to help them make it safely to Gloucestershire.

Lawson (*Dead Cert*). Young farmer with a horse box for hire; Alan York identifies it as the horse box used in the attack on him by a gang of thugs.

Lawson-Young, George (*Shattered*). A professor of respiratory medicine who is working on a very important project in a high-security lab in Bristol. Adam Force formerly worked in the lab, and stole secret data from them.

Leeds, Felicity (*High Stakes*). Wife of Jody; she works together with her husband to steer clients toward crooked bookmaker Ganser Mays.

Leeds, Jody (*High Stakes*). Crooked trainer of Steven Scott's racehorses. Steven takes the horses away from Jody, with dire personal results.

Leeds, Quintus (*High Stakes*). Jody's father; he owns a few racehorses and hates Steven Scott with a passion.

Lees, Wynn (*Comeback*). A racehorse owner with a history of viciousness toward his livestock, he seems particularly eager to blame Ken McClure for problems with his horses. Peter Darwin thinks he's actually disappointed when one of his mares doesn't die while under McClure's care.

Leggatt, Sam (*Break In*). Editor of the scandal sheet *The Daily Flag*, he runs articles that nearly ruin the reputation of Kit Fielding's brother-in-law, Bobby Allardeck.

Lenny (*For Kicks*). A former Borstal boy who is a lad in the stables of Hedley Humber.

Lewis (*Driving Force*). One of Freddie Croft's drivers. He helps the neighboring children with their pet rabbits.

Lily (*Straight*). One of the employees of Saxony Franklin, she looks "like a Charlotte Bronte governess."

Lincoln, Charlotte, aka Charlie (*Smokescreen*). Link's wife.

Lincoln, Chris (*Smokescreen*). Son of Edward Lincoln.

Lincoln, Edward, aka Link (*Smokescreen*). The hero. He is a famous English actor in action films, and is married to Charlie, with two sons, Peter and Chris, and a retarded daughter, Libby. He goes to South Africa to help out his old family friend, Nerissa Cavesey, by checking out the condition of her racehorses there.

Lincoln, Libby (*Smokescreen*). The mentally retarded daughter of Edward Lincoln.

Lincoln, Peter (*Smokescreen*). Son of Edward Lincoln.

Lipton, Lorna (*Driving Force*). Sister to Maudie Watermead, and a relentlessly earnest do-gooder. She teams up with John Tigwood to find homes for aged racehorses.

Litsi, Prince (*Bolt*). Nephew of the Princess Casilia de Brescou, he appears to be Kit Fielding's rival for the affections of Danielle de Brescou. Despite this, Kit finds him likable and a strong ally against Henri Nanterre.

Liv (*Slay-Ride*). Four-year-old in Oslo whose curiosity saves Dave Cleveland from a nasty surprise.

Loder, Nicholas (*Straight*). A highly successful racehorse trainer, he runs Greville Franklin's two horses, Gemstones and Dozen Roses, out of his stables. He is very anxious to sell Dozen Roses to another of his owners, causing Derek Franklin to ponder just why the sale is so important.

Lodge, Inspector (*Dead Cert*). Policeman in Maidenhead given charge of the investigation into Bill Davidson's accident.

Lodovski, Chub (*Blood Sport*). Stud groom at Dave Teller's stud farm in Kentucky.

Logan, Gerard (*Shattered*). The hero. Gerard is a glassblower who owns a shop in the tourist town of Broadway. He is close friends with jockey Martin Stukely, who dies in a fall in the opening scene of the novel.

Longerman, Moira (*Risk*). "Small, blonde, and birdlike," she is the owner of Tapestry, and she insists, against the trainer's protests, that Roland Britten rides her horse in an important race.

Loricroft, George (*Second Wind*). A top racehorse trainer who is friendly with Robin Darcy and Caspar Harvey. He pays little attention to his wife, and travels around Europe quite a bit.

Loricroft, Glenda (*Second Wind*). Married to George, Glenda looks ditsy but is smarter than she appears. She is convinced that George is cheating on her, and asks Perry Stuart to help her. "Every time Glenda spoke, her dominating husband either contradicted or interrupted her."

Lorrimore, Mercer (*The Edge*). Paterfamilias of the rich and privileged Lorrimore family. A genuinely decent man, if overly indulgent.

Lorrimore, Sheridan (*The Edge*). Mercer's son, a thoroughly bad sort.

Lorrimore, Xanthe (*The Edge*). Mercer's daughter, spoiled but not evil.

Losenwoldt, Pieter (*Smokescreen*). A mining engineer who takes Link Lincoln and his colleagues down the Rojedda Reef gold mine.

Louders-Allen-Croft, Lady Emma (*Trial Run*). Prickly girlfriend of Randall Drew. She is an aristocrat who would prefer to be working class.

Ludville, Mrs. Angelisa ("Raid at Kingdom Hill," *Field of Thirteen*). Divorced and unhappy, plagued by a stack of unpaid bills, she sells Tricksy Wilcox two Tote tickets on an important race day.

Lund, Erik (*Slay-Ride*). A journalist who serves as a driver for Dave Cleveland during part of his investigation in Norway. Brother of the policeman, Knut Lund. His dog, a Great Dane named Odin, goes memorably along for the rides. His information on various persons involved in the case proves invaluable to Dave.

Lyon, Thomas (*Wild Horses*). Hero. A young film director, he is working on a film with blockbuster potential, based on the true story of an unsolved crime which scandalized the British racing world twenty-six years before.

Macclesfield, Sir Stuart (*For Kicks*). Steward of the National Hunt Committee, who along with his co-stewards employs Daniel Roke as an undercover investigator. Elderly, tall, with "riotous" white hair.

Mackintosh, Mac (*Comeback*). Now elderly and infirm, he was once a successful trainer in Cheltenham. After listening to his rambling conversation, Peter Darwin is able to piece together part of the story of an old tragedy that has set in motion the present-day crisis for Ken McClure.

Mackintosh, Zoe (*Comeback*). A woman trainer who has taken over for her elderly father. She believes Peter Darwin, despite some initial misgivings, when he tells her about the conspiracy to ruin Ken McClure's reputation.

Macrahinish (*High Stakes*). He is a vet who has been struck off and banned from racecourses.

Margaret (*Bonecrack*). Secretary at Rowley Lodge stables.

Marigold (*Dead Cert*). Dispatcher at Marconicars, a Brighton taxi service.

Martin, Miss Zanna (*Odds Against*). Secretary to the stockbroker Ellis Bolt. Her face has been badly burned in a fire, and she tries as much as possible to hide it from people's view. Sid Halley cultivates her for information, but his professional quest turns to friendship and encouragement of her in her disability. In turn, her quiet courage helps him deal with his own handicap.

Mason, Sandy (*Dead Cert*). Jockey who is not above playing dirty tricks on his fellow jockeys and earning money in underhanded ways.

Mathews, Art (*Nerve*). The opening sentence of *Nerve* is: "Art Mathews shot himself, loudly and messily, in the center of the parade ring at Dunstable races." Art is a senior jockey who finds suicide the only way out of his troubles.

Matthews, Maisie (*In the Frame*). She is a rich widow whose house has just burned down. She has recently returned from a trip to Australia, where she bought a painting by Munnings. The parallels between her experience and that of his cousin Donald Stuart and Donald's wife Regina are too strong for Charles Todd to ignore.

Maudsley, Russell ("Collision Course," *Field of Thirteen*). Co-owner of a newspaper conglomerate, along with Mrs. Robin Dawkins and F. Harold Field.

Mavis (*Dead Cert*). Talkative receptionist at the Pavilion Plaza hotel in Brighton who gives Alan York some information on Clifford Tudor.

Mays, Ganser (*High Stakes*). A crooked bookie who works in conjunction with trainer Jody Leeds to fleece unwary racehorse owners.

McClure, Josephine (*Comeback*). The mother of Ken McClure and the widow of Kenny, the supposed suicide.

McClure, Ken (*Comeback*). He is a highly skilled veterinary surgeon whose specialty is horses. A member of a successful veterinary practice in Cheltenham, he finds his reputation under fire after several horses in his care die not long after he has operated on them. His father, Kenny McClure, had also been a veterinarian who acted as the surgeon at the Cheltenham races, and he killed himself when Ken was a child.

McGregor, Gerard (*Proof*). A private eye who works with Tony Beach on the swapped-liquor scam.

McInnes, Louise (*Whip Hand*). Jenny Halley's roommate in her Oxford flat. Louise meets Sid Halley when he starts his investigation of Nicholas Ashe, and she is pleasantly surprised by how attractive he is. She is a student, writing her thesis.

McLachlan, Alex (*The Edge*). A disgruntled ex–baggage handler for VIA Rail in Canada.

Melbourne Smith, Mr. ("Bright White Star," *Field of Thirteen*). Wheeler-dealer and owner of many racehorses, he is unhappy about the theft of one of his colts.

Mellit, Claudius (*Nerve*). A psychiatrist that Rob Finn consults after he is accused of losing his nerve.

Mervyn, Mrs. (*Dead Cert*). Owner whose horse Alan York rides to victory during the race in which Alan's friend Bill Davidson has his accident.

Mevagissey, Mrs. (*Second Wind*). She is Perry Stuart's beloved grandmother, who raised him after his parents died when he was a child. She was a travel writer, and now that she is wheelchair-bound, she still writes travel guides for the disabled.

Michaels, Gordon (*Banker*). Tim Ekaterin's boss at the Paul Ekaterin Bank Ltd. Husband of Judith. At the beginning of the novel, he has hallucinations and acts strangely due to taking new medication for Parkinson's disease.

Michaels, Judith (*Banker*). Wife of Tim Ekaterin's boss. Tim is in love with her, but she won't do anything to hurt or betray her husband.

Miles, Mason (*Twice Shy*). Owner of the firm where Peter Keithly works.

Millace, George (*Reflex*). Racing photographer who has died in a car accident as the novel begins. Described as a man who liked to catch others in their most humiliating moments, he pays the ultimate price for exercising power over his victims.

Millace, Marie (*Reflex*). Widow of George and mother of Stephen. She is brutally attacked twice and has her house burned down as a result of her husband's unusual activities.

Millace, Steve/Stephen (*Reflex*). Young jockey and a friend of Philip Nore. Because he asks Philip for assistance, Philip finds himself embroiled in a dangerous situation brought about by George Millace's death.

Millbrook, Red ("Dead on Red," *Field of Thirteen*). The beloved English jockey who is the target of a professional assassin.

Miller, Mort (*Twice Shy*). One of Luke Houston's trainers.

Millington, John (*The Edge*). Jockey Club official and Tor Kelsey's boss.

Mills, Kevin (*Come to Grief*). A journalist at a scurrilous tabloid newspaper called *The Pump*.

Mitcham, Dr. (*Dead Cert*). Young physician who attends to Alan York after his accident on Brighton racecourse.

Mohammed, Mr. (*Bolt*). An international arms dealer who supplies Kit Fielding and Prince Litsi with some basic information on the arms trade.

Moncrieff (*Wild Horses*). The director of photography who is working with Thomas Lyon on the movie.

Morden, Margaret (*To the Hilt*). The financial expert that Alexander Kinloch brings in to help with the bankruptcy proceedings of the King Alfred Brewery.

Morris, Alan (*Decider*). Lee's nine-year-old son, who has "freckles and a grin . . . and a deficient sense of danger."

Morris, Amanda (*Decider*). Lee's wife, who has fallen out of love with him. She does love having babies, though.

Morris, Cassandra, aka Cassie (*Twice Shy*). William Derry's girlfriend.

Morris, Christopher (*Decider*). At fourteen the oldest of Lee's sons, he is the mature and responsible one.

Morris, Edward (*Decider*). Lee's ten-year-old son. He is imaginative and quiet.

Morris, Jamie (*Decider*). Lee's ten-month-old son.

Morris, Lee (*Decider*). The hero. He is an architect who restores old ruins and creates beautiful homes from them. He owns shares in Stratton Park racecourse, and is considered a dangerous enemy by the loopy and violent Stratton family.

Morris, Madeline (*Decider*). Lee's mother, who was unhappily married to Keith Stratton. She divorced him and married Leyton Morris, who fathered Lee. Madeline was beaten and raped by Keith while they were married.

Morris, Neil (*Decider*). Lee's seven-year-old son. "Little bright-eyed Neil" is shy and nervous but observant. He clings to his father's hand, and remembers words and phrases that are new to him.

Morris, Toby (*Decider*). Lee's twelve-year-old son, who is a constant worry to his father. Toby unwittingly plays a crucial role in the story.

Morton, Luke-John (*Forfeit*). Irascible sports editor for the *Sunday Blaze* and Ty Tyrone's boss. Definitely a company man, he pushes his reporters to get the good dirt on behalf of the *Blaze*.

Nader, Aziz (*Driving Force*). A new driver and mechanic who arrives on the scene after Freddie Croft's mechanic Jogger is killed.

Nagle, Dennis (*10 Lb. Penalty*). The deceased Member of Parliament whose seat George Juliard is trying to win.

Nagle, Orinda (*10 Lb. Penalty*). Widow of the late Member of Parliament, Dennis Nagle, whose seat George Juliard is attempting to win. Orinda had wanted the seat for herself and at first is highly outraged that the party is supporting Juliard instead of her, and she does her best to derail Juliard's campaign.

Nagrebb, Mr. (*Comeback*). He, along with his vicious son, has a reputation for harsh training methods for his racehorses. Peter Darwin witnesses some of them at firsthand and is then menaced by the son.

Nanterre, Henri (*Bolt*). Young French entrepreneur, he is a partner with Roland de Brescou. When he wants to manufacture and export guns, trading upon the de Brescou-Nanterre reputation, Roland de Brescou resists. Nanterre threatens dire consequences if de Brescou does not go along with his plans.

Nantwich, Joe (*Dead Cert*). Jockey with a drinking problem who finds himself in grave danger from his willingness to accept bribes for spiking races.

Nerrity, Dominic (*The Danger*). A three-year-old kidnap victim in England.

Nerrity, John (*The Danger*). Dominic's father, rich and uncaring.

Nerrity, Miranda (*The Danger*). Mother of Dominic, she is unhappily married to a rich, older man.

Newton, Audrey (*To the Hilt*). Sister of Norman Quorn.

Nigel (*Banker*). Head lad at Oliver Knowles's stud farm.

Nigel (*Driving Force*). One of Freddie Croft's drivers. He is intensely sexy.

Noland, Mike (*The Danger*). The trainer for whom Alessia Cenci often rides when she is in England.

Nore, Amanda (*Reflex*). The younger half sister of Philip Nore. Until his grandmother asks him to find the girl, Philip had no idea she existed.

Nore, Caroline (*Reflex*). Feckless "butterfly" and mother of Philip, who abandoned him in childhood, depositing him with various friends over the years. Philip speculates that she must have died by the time he turned eighteen.

Nore, James (*Reflex*). Son of Lavinia Nore, whom she wishes to disinherit, because she disapproves of his lifestyle.

Nore, Lavinia (*Reflex*). Wealthy grandmother of Philip Nore, who asks his help in finding his hitherto unknown younger half sister, Amanda.

Nore, Philip (*Reflex*). The hero. At the age of thirty, Philip has never had a particularly distinguished career as a steeplechase jockey, although he makes a living at it. Often abandoned by his mother for weeks at a time and left with complaisant friends, he was completely on his own by the time he was eighteen. From one of his informal foster parents, a gay photographer named Charlie, he learned the basics of photography and has developed his skills since, though he doesn't account his abilities as a photographer very high. When he becomes aware that the death of a racing photographer, George Millace, has left Millace's wife and son in a dangerous situation, he tries to decipher the photographic puzzles Millace left behind. In doing so, he endangers his own life.

North, Ronnie (*Knockdown*). A bloodstock agent with whom Jonah Dereham does business in an attempt to buy a horse for Mrs. Kerry Sanders.

Norwood, Chris (*Twice Shy*). An employee of a business involved in the mass production of food in Newmarket, he steals Liam O'Rorke's notes, then gets in trouble when he runs afoul of someone on the trail of the missing computer program for handicapping horses.

Nutbourne, Annabel (*Comeback*). An employee of the British Jockey Club, she is escorting some visiting Japanese dignitaries at Cheltenham racetrack when Peter Darwin first meets her. He is immediately smitten, and he helps her with her Japanese guests by using his skills in Japanese, since she doesn't speak the language and her guests don't speak English.

Nutbridge, Bob ("Corkscrew," *Field of Thirteen*). Young son of Sandy Nutbridge.

Nutbridge, Miranda ("Corkscrew," *Field of Thirteen*). Young daughter of Sandy Nutbridge.

Nutbridge, Mrs. (*"Corkscrew," Field of Thirteen*). Mother of Sandy Nutbridge, she brings her grandchildren from England to Florida to visit their father.

Nutbridge, Sandy (*"Corkscrew," Field of Thirteen*). An agent for a bloodstock agency, he makes a fateful sale to Jules Reginald Harlow, and when he becomes the innocent victim of a vicious scam, he finds a most unexpected ally.

Nyembezi, Piano (*Smokescreen*). A worker at the Rojedda Reef gold mine who delays the scheduled dynamite blasting when he insists that one man in the party of visitors has been left behind down in the mine. He saves Link Lincoln's life.

Oakley, David (*Enquiry*). A corrupt private investigator who provides much of the frame-up of Kelly Hughes.

October, Earl of (*For Kicks*). Steward of the National Hunt Committee who hires Daniel Roke to go undercover to discover who has been doping racehorses with a drug that is undetectable. Father of Lady Elinor and Lady Patricia Tarren.

Offen, Culham James (*Blood Sport*). Owner of Orpheus Farm in California whose niece and nephew, Yola and Matt Clive, have been indulging in some criminous behavior. Known as Uncle Bark to his young relatives.

O'Flaherty, Paddy (*Slay-Ride*). An Irish stable lad in Gunnar Holth's stables. A friend of the missing jockey, Bob Sherman, he is able to provide Dave Cleveland with some important information.

Ogden, Kevin Keith (*Driving Force*). A hitchhiker who dies in one of Freddie Croft's horse vans.

Ogden, Lynn Melissa (*Driving Force*). Kevin Keith's widow; she tells Freddie Croft some crucial information at the inquest into her husband's death.

O'Hara (*Wild Horses*). The film company executive and producer who is overseeing production of Thomas Lyon's movie.

Oldfield, Grant (*Nerve*). A jockey who is not getting many rides anymore, since he lost a job with trainer James Axminster. He is "consumed by some inner rage" against the loss of his career, and eventually he has a nervous breakdown.

O'Rorke, Liam (*Twice Shy*). Deceased professional gambler, he developed the system for handicapping that Peter Keithly was able to turn into a computer program.

O'Rorke, Mrs. (*Twice Shy*). The widow of professional gambler Liam O'Rorke, she hopes Jonathan Derry can find the missing program so that she can turn it over to Harry Gilbert, who paid a lot of money for it.

Osborn, Ramsey (*Hot Money*). Wealthy, congenial American racehorse owner, he and Malcolm Pembroke instantly become cronies. He serves as an enthusiastic guide as Malcolm becomes more acquainted with the world of high-stakes racing. He is coowner of the horse Blue Clancy, along with Malcolm.

Osborne, Harold (*Reflex*). Trainer out of whose stable Philip Nore often rides. Osborne trains the horses of Victor Briggs, one of Philip's most frequent employers.

Osprey, Norman (*Shattered*). A bookie who looks like a fat Elvis Presley, and works for the Arthur Robins bookmaking firm. He is in cahoots with Rose Payne to find the moneymaking videotape.

Ostermeyer, Martha (*Straight*). The wife of wealthy American race-horse owner Harley Ostermeyer, she is the quiet power behind the throne.

O'Tree, Terence (*Reflex*). A man who shot five horses belonging to Elgin Yaxley. He served time in prison for the offense, but officials could never prove that Yaxley paid him to do it so he could collect the insurance money.

Ownslow (*Risk*). With his partner Glitberg, he ran a construction racket that bilked the unwary of untold millions, until he was bested by Roland Britten.

Oxon, Captain (*Odds Against*). The manager of Seabury racecourse.

Paddy (*For Kicks*). Stable lad in the Earl of October's stables. Forty; a tough, sharp Irishman who seldom misses a trick.

Palissey, Mrs. (*Proof*). She works as a shop assistant in Tony Beach's wine shop, along with her retarded nephew Brian.

Palmerstone, Cinders (*Driving Force*). The nine-year-old daughter of Freddie Croft and Susan Palmerstone. She doesn't know that Freddie is her biological father.

Palmerstone, Hugo (*Driving Force*). Married to Susan, he suspects that she and Freddie once had an affair and that his daughter Cinders was really fathered by Freddie. He declares himself to be Freddie's enemy.

Palmerstone, Susan (*Driving Force*). Freddie Croft used to ride her father's horses, and they had an affair long ago. She had his child but passed it off as her husband's.

Panake, Lew (*Dead Cert*). Well-dressed bookmaker who takes Alan York's occasional bets.

Pankhurst, Pip (*Nerve*). He is the chief stable jockey for James Axminster; Rob Finn is hired as second to Pip. When Pip breaks his leg, Rob is offered Pip's ride and does so well that Axminster takes him on as Pip's replacement—a major promotion in Rob's career.

Pannier, Dorothea (*Wild Horses*). An elderly woman, she is the sister of Valentine Clark and is taking care of him in his last illness. She is viciously attacked and almost killed by thugs who are after something that her brother had.

Pannier, Paul (*Wild Horses*). The officious son of Dorothea Pannier, he is hostile to Tom Lyon, but he gets his comeuppance in a nasty manner.

Pargetter, Ian (*Banker*). A vet who works closely with Calder Jackson, and refers sick horses to him for unorthodox methods of healing.

Parlane, Jed (*To the Hilt*). He is the factor on the Earl of Kinloch's Scottish estate, and a good friend of Alexander Kinloch.

Patrick (*Flying Finish*). A kind and humorous cargo pilot with whom Henry Grey flies several flights, including crucial ones to Milan. He introduces Henry to Gabriella Barzini.

Payne, Eddie (*Shattered*). Martin Stukely's racecourse valet, who delivers a mysterious videotape to Gerard Logan. He is also the father of the sociopathic Rose Payne, who loves to inflict pain on men.

Payne, Rose (*Shattered*). Rose is the daughter of valet Eddie Payne; she works for the bookmaking firm of Arthur Robins. She likes to be known as Mrs. Robins, although she's never been married and there has never been a Mr. Robins. Rose hates men, and she has wildly violent impulses, especially when she doesn't get her own way.

Peaky (*Dead Cert*). Thug; part of a group who delivers a nasty message to Alan York to mind his own business.

Pembroke, Alicia (*Hot Money*). First mistress, then later third wife of Malcolm Pembroke, she is the mother of Gervase, Ferdinand, and Serena. She is bitter over Malcolm's treatment of her and her children, and she does her best to keep things stirred up, with everyone at odds with everyone else.

Pembroke, Berenice (*Hot Money*). A nasty, nagging sort of woman, she is married to Thomas, whom she belittles at every possible turn.

Pembroke, Coochie (*Hot Money*). The deceased fourth wife of Malcolm Pembroke and mother of the twins, Robin and Peter, the latter of whom died in the accident that claimed Coochie's life. A motherly woman, she had served as a surrogate mother to Ian.

Pembroke, Deborah, aka Debs (*Hot Money*). A beautiful model, she is married to Ferdinand.

Pembroke, Donald (*Hot Money*). The eldest son of Malcolm Pembroke, by his first wife, Vivien. Married to Helen, he is secretary at a prestigious golf club at Henley-on-Thames. Status is everything to him, and he is bitterly resentful over his treatment by his father.

Pembroke, Edwin né Bugg (*Hot Money*). A spineless, parasitic type, married to Lucy. He was easily persuaded to give up his own name, Bugg, in favor of his wife's, in order to curry favor with his wealthy father-in-law.

Pembroke, Ferdinand (*Hot Money*). An illegitimate son of Malcolm Pembroke and his mistress (and later third wife), Alicia. A year younger than Ian, he is the most like his father in looks and temperament. He seems not to mind the stigma of illegitimacy as much as his brother Gervase and has managed to establish himself successfully in his career as a statistician in an insurance company, and is studying to be an actuary. He is married to the beautiful Deborah, a model.

Pembroke, Gervase (*Hot Money*). An illegitimate son of Malcolm Pembroke and his mistress (and later third wife), Alicia. Despite being acknowledged and adopted by his father, so that he legally bears the Pembroke name, Gervase nurses a grudge against Ian, whom he perceives as Malcolm's favorite. A stockbroker by profession, he is married to Ursula and is the father of two daughters.

Pembroke, Helen (*Hot Money*). The beautiful and reputedly brainless wife of Donald, Malcolm Pembroke's eldest son. She makes some money by doing china painting and is the mother of one daughter who no longer lives at home and twin sons in their first term at Eton.

Pembroke, Ian (*Hot Money*). The hero. The fifth child (and third son) of wealthy gold trader Malcolm Pembroke, Ian is an amateur jockey. He is apparently the only one among the extended family whom his father trusts, when Malcolm Pembroke insists that a member of the family is trying to kill him. Though he is estranged from most of his siblings (not to mention their mothers), he is also the only one who seems to love Malcolm unreservedly, and he undertakes to investigate, trying to figure out who wants Malcolm dead the most.

Pembroke, Joyce (*Hot Money*). Malcolm Pembroke's second wife, she is the mother of Ian. After her divorce from Malcolm, she becomes a highly successful tournament bridge player and teacher.

Pembroke, Lucy (*Hot Money*). Elder daughter and second child of Malcolm Pembroke, by his first wife Vivien. A poetess fallen on lean times, she is married to the parasitic Edwin Bugg, whom she persuaded to take her own surname, apparently not enamored of being known as Lucy Bugg. She has one teenage son.

Pembroke, Malcolm (*Hot Money*). Highly successful gold trader with a penchant for marrying and the father of nine children, with eight living. Convinced that one of the family is trying to kill him, he turns to his third son, Ian, for protection.

Pembroke, Moira (*Hot Money*). Ill-fated fifth wife of Malcolm Pembroke. Her murder brings an end to the estrangement between Malcolm and his third son, Ian.

Pembroke, Robin (*Hot Money*). The youngest son of Malcolm Pembroke, he lives permanently in special care, after a car accident which claimed the life of his mother, Coochie, and his twin brother, Peter.

Pembroke, Serena (*Hot Money*). Seventh child and youngest daughter of

Malcolm Pembroke by his third wife, Alicia. She would love to be Daddy's girl, but Malcolm keeps pushing her away.

Pembroke, Thomas (*Hot Money*). Second son and third child of Malcolm Pembroke, by his first wife Vivien. A somewhat colorless man, he is married to the sharp-tongued Berenice.

Pembroke, Vivien (*Hot Money*). The somewhat colorless first wife of Malcolm Pembroke, and the mother of Donald, Lucy, and Thomas.

Penn, Deb (*Dead Cert*). Snobbish aunt of Kate Ellery-Penn, wife of George Penn.

Penn, George (*Dead Cert*). Uncle of Kate Ellery-Penn who gives her a racehorse, Heavens Above. Mastermind behind the scheme to fix races and owner of a taxi service, which is a cover for an extortion racket in Brighton.

Pentelow, Evan (*Smokescreen*). The sadistic and sardonic director of a film in which Link Lincoln is starring, *Man in a Car*.

Perryside, Lucy (*Break In*). Wife of Major Clement Perryside.

Perryside, Major Clement (*Break In*). He once owned the racehorse, Metavane, until he met Maynard Allardeck.

Peter(*Risk*). A sullen assistant in the accountancy firm in which Roland Britten is junior partner.

Petrovich, Clay ("The Gift," *Field of Thirteen*). Journalist and associate of Fred Collyer's, who gives Fred rides to and from Churchill Downs.

Picton, Norman (*Come to Grief*). A detective inspector on the Thames Valley police force.

Pigeon, Tom (*Shattered*). An ex-con with three menacing dobermans; Gerard Logan hires him for bodyguard duty. He is "known locally as 'The Backlash' chiefly on account of being as quick with his wits as his fists."

Pinlock, Hilary Margaret (*Risk*). A no-nonsense middle-aged schoolmistress, she provides a rescue more than once for Roland Britten. She asks only one thing in return, and Roland grants it, albeit with some misgivings.

Pitts, Jane (*Twice Shy*). The wife of Ted Pitts, she puts William Derry in touch with a computer expert, Ruth Quigley.

Pitts, Ted (*Twice Shy*). A mathematics master at Jonathan Derry's school, he has the necessary computer know-how to help Jonathan decipher the computer program for handicapping horses. Later on, he reluctantly assists William Derry as William attempts to bring about a final solution to the mess the computer program has caused.

Pollgate, Nestor (*Break In*). Owner of the *Daily Flag*, he uses his paper as a battering ram to get what he wants, not caring whom he destroys in the process.

Polly (*10 Lb. Penalty*). Known chiefly as "Dearest Polly," she is a well-connected woman who is firmly on George Juliard's side in his bid to become a Member of Parliament. She and Ben Juliard develop a warm relationship, and Ben is pleased when she eventually becomes his stepmother.

Poole, Inky (*Whip Hand*). George Caspar's work jockey.

Porter (*In the Frame*). A large plainclothes Australian policeman who meets Charles Todd and Jik and Sarah Cassavetes in Melbourne.

Powys, Connaught (*Risk*). A businessman with a talent for embezzling, he went to jail, thanks to Roland Britten. He swore vengeance on Roland, and Roland fears Powys may be behind the attacks on him.

Prensela, Walt (*Blood Sport*). An investigator for the Buttress Life Insurance company who has been working on the case of Dave Teller's missing racehorse, Chrysalis. Though at first suspicious of Gene Hawkins's abilities to succeed where he himself has so far failed, he becomes a friend of Gene's, and it is through him that Gene eventually succeeds in overcoming his depression.

Prime Minister (*10 Lb. Penalty*). Though he is never named otherwise, this important political figure meets with Ben and George Juliard to discuss their concerns about the power-hungry machinations of A. L. Wyvern.

Pucinelli, Enrico (*The Danger*). The Italian policeman who helps Andrew Douglas on the Cenci kidnapping.

Pyle, Billy (*In the Frame*). He introduces Charles Todd to Maisie Matthews, thus starting the investigative road down which Charles travels to Australia in search of Regina Stuart's killers.

Quayle, Oliver (*Whip Hand*). Admiral Roland's solicitor, who is giving advice on Jenny Halley's legal problems.

Quentin, Daffodil (*The Edge*). A dodgy Canadian racehorse owner. She owns a half share in a horse with Filmer.

Quest, Harold (*Decider*). An animal-rights protestor at the Stratton Park racecourse. He holds a sign saying: "Horses Rights Come First." He becomes a suspect when somebody blows up the racecourse stands.

Quigley, Miles (*Proof*). The caterer at Martineau Park racecourse.

Quigley, Oliver (*Second Wind*). A racehorse trainer who seems congenitally nervous. He is "temperamentally unsuited to any stressful way of life, let alone the nerve-breaking day-to-day of the thoroughbred circuit." He trains Caspar Harvey's horses, and is friendly with Robin Darcy.

Quigley, Ruth (*Twice Shy*). A computer whiz, she was once a student of Ted Pitts. William Derry consults her when he is trying to decipher Peter Keithly's computer program.

Quince, Rose (*Break In*). Reporter working for Lord Vaughnley on the *Towncrier*, she shows Kit Fielding a videotape that helps him find a way out of the volatile situation surrounding his sister and brother-in-law.

Quincy, Oliver (*Comeback*). A general large-animal vet who does minor surgery with Carey Hewett's veterinary practice. Of the more junior partners, he seems the one most eager to dump Hewett and set up a new practice when repeated disasters compromise their reputation under Hewett's leadership.

Quint, Ellis (*Come to Grief*). A famous television broadcaster and old friend of Sid Halley's. Ellis formerly was an outstanding amateur steeplechase jockey, and rode many races against Sid. Now he is accused by Sid of maiming horses, and the great British public is sure that he's innocent and Sid is wrong.

Quint, Ginnie (*Come to Grief*). Ellis's mother. She is a gentle soul, who can't believe that anyone close to her could be evil.

Quint, Gordon (*Come to Grief*). Ellis's father, and a gentleman farmer. At the opening of the novel, he attacks Sid Halley with a metal bar and breaks his arm.

Quipp, Professor (*Driving Force*). Lizzie Croft's latest lover. He is a professor of organic chemistry in Edinburgh.

Quorn, Norman (*To the Hilt*). He was the finance director of the King Alfred Brewery. He has embezzled the company's money and disappeared.

Radnor (*Odds Against*). He owns Hunt Radnor Associates, and is Sid Halley's boss.

Rammileese, Mark (*Whip Hand*). Peter's young son, who innocently helps Sid Halley and Chico Barnes escape from a dreadful situation.

Rammileese, Peter (*Whip Hand*). A farmer who forms syndicates to buy horses, and then manipulates them. He's "made a packet out of crooked dealings in horses . . . he'll try to bribe anyone from the Senior Steward to the scrubbers, and where he can't bribe, he threatens."

Ramsey, Detective Superintendent (*Comeback*). From the Gloucestershire police, he is investigating the murderous goings-on at Carey Hewett's veterinary practice in Cheltenham.

Ramsey, Rupert (*High Stakes*). Steven Scott moves his racehorses Energise, Dial, and Ferryboat to Ramsey's stables after taking them away from trainer Jody Leeds.

Randolph, Sophie (*Knockdown*). An air traffic controller, she meets Jonah Dereham in the aftermath of a car accident, caused when one of his horses escapes and runs loose.

Ranger, Rinty (*Slay-Ride*). English jockey who often races in Norway; he fills Dave Cleveland in on some key information about the missing jockey, Bob Sherman.

Reggie (*For Kicks*). Food-stealing lad in the stables of Hedley Humber.

Reilly, Moggie ("Haig's Death," *Field of Thirteen*). A jump jockey, he's all set to ride at Winchester Spring Meeting, but an affair with Sarah Driffield causes some interesting complications.

Renbo, Harley (*In the Frame*). The gallery keeper at the Yarra River Gallery in Alice Springs. He is also a painter himself, and he is proud to show Charles Todd his own paintings.

Retsov, Martin ("Nightmare," *Field of Thirteen*). Haunted by his father's death during a horse theft three years before, he decides to revert to his old profession when the seemingly perfect assistant comes along. But sometimes fate has a way of playing cruel tricks, as Martin Retsov will discover.

Rich, Jericho (*Driving Force*). A "loud, aggressive, and impatient" racehorse owner and client of Freddie Croft.

Richmond, Nell (*The Edge*). She is the coordinator of the Great Transcontinental Mystery Racing Train trip, and travels on the train herself. Tor Kelsey falls in love with her.

Ridger, Sergeant John (*Proof*). The rigidly upright and proper policeman with whom Tony Beach goes wine tasting.

Rivera, Alessandro, aka Alex (*Bonecrack*). Immature and lacking in experience, only eighteen years old, he is hopeful of riding the favorite Archangel in the Derby, thanks to his father's methods of extortion.

Rivera, Enso (*Bonecrack*). Gangster who forces Neil Griffon to allow his son, Alessandro, to ride the Derby hopeful, Archangel, who is trained at Rowley Lodge stables. He threatens to destroy the stables and the elder Griffon's livelihood and reputation if Neil doesn't comply with his orders.

Robbitson, Dr. Keith (*To the Hilt*). Sir Ivan Westering's busy and formidably competent doctor, who also takes care of Alexander Kinloch after he's been injured.

Roberts, Derek ("Spring Fever," *Field of Thirteen*). A handsome young jockey, he is the object of affection of owner Mrs. Angela Hart and participates in a scheme to defraud her.

Robinson, Bill (*Wild Horses*). A young motorcycle mechanic who is a friend of Dorothea Pannier's. Dorothea had asked him to safeguard her brother's library, thus saving it from her own son, who'd like to make sure Thomas Lyon never receives this legacy from Valentine Clark.

Robson, Detective Inspector (*Twice Shy*). The officer assisting Detective Chief Superintendent Irestone in the investigation into the murder of Chris Norwood.

Rockman, Davey, aka The Rock ("Dead on Red," *Field of Thirteen*).

Demoted from his position as star jockey, he is jealous enough of Red Millbrook's success to want him dead.

Roke, Belinda (*For Kicks*). Younger sister of Daniel Roke. She wants to attend medical school.

Roke, Daniel (*For Kicks*). The hero. Young owner of a prosperous stud farm in Australia; he has three younger siblings, Belinda, Helen, and Philip, to whom he acts as a father after their parents' death. He goes undercover in the racing stables of Hedley Humber to uncover the ring behind the doping of racehorses with a seemingly new and undetectable drug.

Roke, Helen (*For Kicks*). Younger sister of Daniel Roke. She wants to attend art school.

Roke, Philip (*For Kicks*). Younger brother of Daniel Roke. He is thirteen and would like to become a lawyer.

Roland, Rear Admiral Charles (*Odds Against*; *Whip Hand*; *Come to Grief*). Sid Halley's father-in-law, who sets him on the road to recovery after he's been shot. He provides a refuge and help for Sid whenever he needs it.

Rollo, Mr. (*Dead Cert*). Clerk of the course at the West Sussex races.

Rollway, Thomas, aka Rollo (*Straight*). A racehorse owner with a penchant for violence who seems particularly insistent on buying Greville Franklin's horse, Dozen Roses.

Romney, William (*Slay-Ride*). Grandfather to Emma Sherman who assists his granddaughter and Dave Cleveland in finding out what really happened to the missing Bob Sherman.

Roots, Jefferson L. (*Blood Sport*). Owner of Perry Stud Farm, on whose farm one of the missing stallions is eventually "found."

Roper, Arnold, aka Bob Smith ("Blind Chance," *Field of Thirteen*). A man with an unusual job, he has an unbeatable system for winning bets at the races, but fate, in the shape of a young blind man, is about to take a hand.

Rose (*Driving Force*). One of Freddie Croft's secretaries.

Roskin, Mr. ("Raid at Kingdom Hill," *Field of Thirteen*). Member of the executive committee at Kingdom Hill Racecourse who derides Bellamy's interest in security for the racecourse.

Ross, Colin (*Rat Race*). A famous champion jockey who is Matt Shore's best client. Brother of Nancy and Midge Ross.

Ross, Midge (*Rat Race*). Nancy's twin sister. She is gravely ill with leukemia.

Ross, Nancy (*Rat Race*). Girlfriend of Matt Shore and sister of Colin Ross. Nancy is learning to fly a light plane; her troubles in flying are the basis for an exciting chase sequence in the novel.

Rous-Wheeler, John (*Flying Finish*). A man who needs transport.

Rourke, Nash (*Wild Horses*). The Hollywood mega-star who has the lead role in Thomas Lyon's movie. He quickly becomes Thomas's ally and is key in helping Thomas keep his job when Howard Tyler does his best to cause trouble.

Rudd, Basil (*10 Lb. Penalty*). Garage owner and cousin of journalist Usher Rudd. He, like the rest of his family, is none too fond of the scandal-mongering member of the clan.

Rudd, Usher, aka Bobby (*10 Lb. Penalty*). A muckraking journalist, he wants to get as much dirt as possible on any public figure, and he and Ben Juliard tangle more than once because Rudd is determined to find dirt on George Juliard.

Rupert (*Dead Cert*). Stable lad.

Rupert (*Banker*). A colleague of Tim Ekaterin's at the bank. Tim and the others cover for him, as he is unable to do much work while his wife is dying.

Rupert, John (*Second Wind*). An antiterrorism agent of the British government. Perry Stuart talks to him in London.

Russell, John (*Dead Cert*). Member of the St. John Ambulance brigade providing assistance at Maidenhead racecourse; in his statement to the police he reveals that he is the first person to reach Bill Davidson after his accident.

Sammy (*Bolt*). Hired muscle who protects the de Brescou household while Henri Nanterre remains a threat.

Sanders, Mrs. Kerry (*Knockdown*). Rich American woman who seeks the services of bloodstock agent Jonah Dereham in her attempt to buy a gift for the son of her fiancé.

Sandvik, Mikkel (*Slay-Ride*). Sixteen-year-old son of the Norwegian businessman, Per Bjorn Sandvik. A friend of the missing jockey, Bob Sherman, Mikkel might hold the key to his disappearance.

Sandvik, Per Bjorn (*Slay-Ride*). Powerful Norwegian businessman and racehorse owner; one of the stewards of the Norwegian Jockey Club. Missing jockey Bob Sherman sometimes stayed with him when he rode in Norway and befriended his son Mikkel.

Schultz, Blisters ("The Gift," *Field of Thirteen*). A pickpocket by trade, he hopes for good pickings at the Kentucky Derby; and with Fred Collyer's wallet in his hands, he hits what looks like a jackpot.

Scott, Clement ("Spring Fever," *Field of Thirteen*). Trainer of Billyboy, belonging to Mrs. Angela Hart, he's not above cheating an owner, even a motherly sort like Mrs. Hart.

Scott, Steven (*High Stakes*). The hero. Steven is an inventor of ingenious wind-up toys called Rola toys. He owns several racehorses but has never spent much time with them until he tries to take his horse Energise away from crooked trainer Jody Leeds.

Searle, Simon (*Flying Finish*). He gives Henry Grey a job at Yardman Transport.

Shacklebury, Paul (*The Edge*). A murdered stable lad.

Shandy, Milo (*Straight*). Racehorse trainer from whose stable Derek Franklin gets many of his rides.

Shell, Simpson (*Twice Shy*). One of Luke Houston's trainers, he is none too keen on William Derry's abilities as a racing manager.

Sherman, Emma (*Slay-Ride*). Distraught, pregnant wife of the missing jockey, Bob Sherman. Dave Cleveland does his best to look after her while he searches for the truth about her husband's disappearance.

Sherman, Robert, aka Bob (*Slay-Ride*). A talented steeplechase jockey, he disappeared after a race in Oslo, apparently having stolen a large sum of money.

Shipton, Henry (*Banker*). Chairman of the merchant bank Paul Ekaterin Ltd. He goes with Tim Ekaterin and Gordon Michaels to the races.

Shore, Matt (*Rat Race*). The hero. An airplane pilot with no interest in racing; he starts working for an air taxi firm, which assigns him passengers going to race meets. He has a checkered past, having given up a plum job with BOAC in order to keep his wife happy, then being blamed unjustly for a commercial flight that strayed badly off course. He is divorced, broke, and lonely.

Shummuck, Barry (*Whip Hand*). Brother of Trevor Deansgate.

Silva (*Wild Horses*). The temperamental and touchy actress who has the female lead in Thomas Lyon's film.

Simmons, Arthur (*For Kicks*). Stable hand on Daniel Roke's farm. The Earl of October intends to offer him the job as undercover agent for the National Hunt Committee before he realizes that Daniel would do a much better job.

Simms (*Straight*). Chauffeur to the Ostermeyers, he has a sticky fate in store.

Simpson, Greg ("Blind Chance," *Field of Thirteen*). Tired of being made redundant, he takes a job with Arnold Roper (whom he knows only as Bob Smith), helping work his fiddle and making good money at it.

Small (*Dead Cert*). Policeman at the enquiry desk at the Maidenhead police station where Alan York goes to report his beating by a group of thugs.

Smith, Bob ("Blind Chance," *Field of Thirteen*). Alias used by Arnold Roper, so Greg Simpson can't easily identify his employer.

Smith, Dissdale (*Banker*). A friend of Calder Jackson. He gambles heavily on races.

Smith, Geoff (*For Kicks*). Lad in the stables of Hedley Humber; forced to leave, as most lads are, after a certain length of time.

Smith, John, aka Gypsy Joe ("Dead on Red," *Field of Thirteen*). The trainer for whom Red Millbrook had achieved stunning success, he is not content until he discovers who was behind the jockey's murder.

Smith, Mr. (*Hot Money*). An expert on incendiary devices, he assists on the investigation into the bombing of Malcolm Pembroke's home, Quantum.

Smith, Peter (*Dead Cert*). Head traveling lad of the Gregory stables, where Bill Davidson's horse Admiral is trained.

Smith, Sandy (*Driving Force*). The village constable of Pixhill.

Sonny (*Dead Cert*). Knife-wielding thug; part of a group who delivers a nasty message to Alan York to mind his own business.

Springwood, Jerry ("The Day of the Losers," *Field of Thirteen*). At thirty-two, he's a jockey who's lost his nerve, but at the Grand National at Aintree, he's going to face a highly unusual race.

Stallworthy, Spencer (*10 Lb. Penalty*). Well-known racehorse trainer who stables and trains a horse that George Juliard buys for Ben as a birthday present.

Stampe, David (*Dead Cert*). Tale-bearing son of the senior steward.

Stampe, Sir Creswell (*Dead Cert*). Senior steward of the National Hunt Committee, to whom Alan York reports his suspicions about Bill Davidson's death.

Stapleton, Tommy (*For Kicks*). Journalist who was killed in a car accident while investigating the doping scheme.

Stirling, C. V. (*Slay-Ride*). A neighbor of Dave Cleveland's, he very handily is a surgeon and provides some medical assistance after Dave survives an attempt on his life.

Stratton, Conrad (*Decider*). Conrad has become Lord Stratton on the death of his father. He is the elder (by a few minutes) of twins, so he inherits the title and the estate. His twin brother is the jealous and violent Keith.

Stratton, Dart (*Decider*). Son of Conrad Stratton and grandson of the old

Lord Stratton. Dart is charming and the most likable member of the Stratton family, but he has little ambition. He is obsessed with the fact that he is going bald, and is constantly looking for a cure for baldness.

Stratton, Forsyth (*Decider*). Ivan's son, and the old Lord Stratton's grandson.

Stratton, Hannah (*Decider*). Daughter of Keith and half sister of Lee Morris. She is bitter and unhappy and has "never done a day's hard work," but she adores her son, Jack.

Stratton, Ivan (*Decider*). The youngest son of the old Lord Stratton. He owns a garden center, and is appreciably less violent than most of the Stratton family.

Stratton, Jack (*Decider*). The illegitimate son of Hannah Stratton and grandson of Keith. "Jack, a loose-lipped teenager, mirrored his grandfather too thoroughly; handsome and mean."

Stratton, Keith (*Decider*). Twin brother of Conrad Stratton. Keith is jealous of his brother, as well as generally violent and impulsive. He is the ex-husband of Lee Morris's mother.

Stratton, Lord (*Decider*). Deceased when the novel begins, he still exerts a powerful influence over his squabbling family.

Stratton, Rebecca (*Decider*). She is a female jockey, and is hard, intense, and violent. Her whole life is racing, and she is intensely ambitious.

Stuart, Donald (*In the Frame*). Charles Todd's cousin, who lives in Shropshire and has a wine business. He comes home one Friday night from work and finds his beautiful young wife Regina dead in their home. He is practically destroyed by grief for her.

Stuart, Perry (*Second Wind*). The hero. Perry has a Ph.D. in physics, and he works as a television meteorologist for the BBC. He was raised by his grandmother after his parents died, and she is the one person with whom he has a very close relationship. He is adventurous, cool-headed, and an excellent swimmer, all qualities that hold him in good stead when his plane goes down over the Caribbean during a hurricane.

Stukely, Bon-Bon (*Shattered*). Martin's "rich, plump and talkative wife."

Stukely, Martin (*Shattered*). A successful, thirty-four-year-old jump jockey and good friend of Gerard Logan. He is killed in a fall at Cheltenham Races on New Year's Eve. His death sets into motion the troubles that come to haunt Gerard.

Sundby, Paul (*Slay-Ride*). Norwegian racehorse trainer who trains the horses of Rolf Torp.

Swann, Lida (*Risk*). Beautiful but vacuous mistress of William Finch.

Swayle, Orkney (*Proof*). An irascible racehorse owner who makes Flora Hawthorn nervous; thus she asks Tony Beach to come with her to the races at Martineau Park near Oxford.

Sylvester, Scott (*Comeback*). A qualified veterinary nurse, he is also the anesthetist who assists at the surgeries when Ken McClure has had equine patients who died after surgery or on the operating table.

Tape, Nigel ("Dead on Red," *Field of Thirteen*). A second-string jockey, he burns with resentment over his mate Davey Rockman's replacement by Red Millbrook.

Tarleton, Thomas N. (*For Kicks*). Nicknamed Soupy or TNT (for his initials); a shady character from Granger's, a racing stable near the Earl of October's stables in Yorkshire.

Tarren, Lady Elinor (*For Kicks*). Elder daughter of the Earl of October and a student at Oxford. Friendlier and less spoiled than her younger sister and brother.

Tarren, Lady Patricia (*For Kicks*). Flirtatious, vindictive daughter of the Earl of October; has a twin brother. When her attempted seduction of Daniel Roke fails, she turns her father against Daniel.

Tatum, Davis (*Come to Grief*). A lawyer who works with Sid Halley during his investigation into Ellis Quint's actions.

Taylor, Hudson (*In the Frame*). Managing director of Monga Vineyards. He did business with Donald Stuart on his trip to Australia. He meets with Charles Todd at the races and talks about Donald's purchase of a Munnings painting.

Teck, Mervyn (*10 Lb. Penalty*). George Juliard's agent, or chief of staff, in his campaign to be elected to Parliament. Though he is a proponent of Orinda Nagle, he does his best to get Juliard elected.

Teddington, Popsy (*The Danger*). Racehorse trainer in England. Alessia Cenci goes to her house to recover after being kidnapped.

Teller, Dave (*Blood Sport*). American millionaire and owner of champion racehorses, he hires Gene Hawkins to discover the whereabouts of his missing horse, Chrysalis. He and Simon Keeble were both involved in intelligence efforts during World War II, which is how they came to know each other.

Teller, Eunice (*Blood Sport*). Millionaire Dave Teller's bored wife, whose alcohol consumption and amorous nature prompt Gene Hawkins to suggest some alternative therapy.

Terence (*For Kicks*). Manservant to the Earl of October, who assists Daniel Roke in his transformation from Australian businessman to seedy English tough.

Terry (*10 Lb. Penalty*). Mechanic at Basil Rudd's garage, who examines George Juliard's Range Rover when Ben Juliard suspects the vehicle has been tampered with.

Teska, Pauli (*Knockdown*). A very successful American bloodstock agent with an overpowering personality, he refers Mrs. Kerry Sanders as a client to Jonah Dereham.

Thiveridge, Claud (*Dead Cert*). Mysterious "chairman" of the group who bought Marconicars from Clifford Tudor.

Thomas (*Bolt; Break In*). Chauffeur for the Princess Casilia de Brescou.

Thomkins (*Dead Cert*). Pub owner who gives Alan York information on the extortion racket in Brighton fronted by a taxi service.

Thrace, Henry (*Whip Hand*). He owns two horses formerly trained by George Caspar, Gleaner and Zingaloo, who were retired from racing when they developed heart problems.

Tigwood, John (*Driving Force*). He is the director of Centaur Care, a charity for pensioned-off steeplechasers.

Tilepit, Lord (*Come to Grief*). He is a friend of Owen Cliff Yorkshire, and on the board of directors of Topline Foods.

Tina (*Straight*). A general assistant at Saxony Franklin.

Titmuss, Tommy (*The Edge*). The character that Tor Kelsey plays in the mystery play being staged on the race train. Tommy is supposed to be a waiter, and Tor even has to do the dishes every night while in character.

Todd, Charles (*In the Frame*). Todd is a painter who specializes in paintings of horses. The brutal murder of his cousin's wife starts him on the trail of a set of vicious art thieves.

Tollman, Marius ("The Gift," *Field of Thirteen*). A man with a knack for staying out of trouble, he's about to work a big scam at the Kentucky Derby, if only Fred Collyer doesn't get in his way.

Tollright, Tobias (*To the Hilt*). He is the auditor who uncovers the embezzlement at the King Alfred Brewery.

Tompkins, Binny (*Risk*). Racehorse trainer who reluctantly puts Roland Britten on Tapestry.

Torp, Rolf (*Slay-Ride*). Norwegian businessman and racehorse owner;

one of the stewards of the Norwegian Jockey Club. Missing jockey Bob Sherman had recently ridden for him.

Tramp ("Bright White Star," *Field of Thirteen*). An unnamed vagabond who thwarts the underhanded scheme of Jim and Vivi Turner.

Trelawney, Elliot (*Straight*). A colleague of Greville Franklin's from the West London Magistrates Court, he needs access to some papers on a case that Greville had been interested in.

Trent, Larry (*Proof*). Owner of a thriving restaurant and bar. He is suspected of switching cheap liquor for expensive brands in an elaborate scheme to defraud customers.

Tudor, Clifford (*Dead Cert*). Owner of a couple of horses, one of whom is Bolingbroke. Joe Nantwich often rides for him. A businessman with shady antecedents and former owner of the Marconicars taxi service in Brighton.

Tunny, Tug (*Break In*). Editor of "Intimate Details" for the *Daily Flag*, which ran scurrilous articles about Bobby Allardeck and his stables.

Turner, Jim ("Bright White Star," *Field of Thirteen*). A stable owner who, along with his wife Vivi, resorts to a desperate measure to make a success of his stable.

Turner, Vivi ("Bright White Star," *Field of Thirteen*). Wife of Jim, with whom she conspires in a daring theft to shore up the fortunes of their faltering stable.

Tyderman, Major (*Rat Race*). One of Matt Shore's passengers on the ill-fated plane trip to Haydock racecourse. "He had thin salt-and-pepper hair brushed sideways across a balding crown and he carried his head stiffly, with his chin tucked back into his neck. Tense: very tense. And wary, looking at the world with suspicion."

Tyler, Howard (*Wild Horses*). A novelist and Oscar-winning screenwriter, he has adapted his own novel for the screen. He is a constant thorn in the side of Tom Lyon because he objects to the changes that Tom insists on making to his work. His attempts to counteract Tom's changes almost cost Tom his job as director of the film.

Tyrone, Elizabeth (*Forfeit*). Wife of James "Ty" Tyrone. Confined to an iron lung, thanks to a bout with polio that has left her helpless to care for herself. Though she tries to put a brave front on things for her husband's sake, she nevertheless realizes what a burden she imposes on her husband.

Tyrone, James (aka Ty) (*Forfeit*). The hero. A racing reporter for one of Britain's popular scandal sheets, the *Sunday Blaze*, Ty is respected among his colleagues, though he sometimes wishes he wrote for a more respectable newspaper. But the *Blaze* pays better than its more staid fellows, and he has some extraordinary expenses. His wife, Elizabeth, after being stricken with polio some years before, is confined to an iron lung and needs a considerable amount of care, for which he has to pay out of his own pocket. In a key scene he is forced to drink until he is inebriated after being beaten by the villain's henchman. Afterward, barely able to stand, he gets his invalid wife out of the house and safely away from any further attempts on her life.

Ullaston, Sir Thomas (*Whip Hand*). The senior steward of the Jockey Club.

Underfield, Bart (*Reflex*). Trainer who likes to seem smarter than he really is. Five horses belonging to Elgin Yaxley were shot to death while under his care.

Unwin (*Second Wind*). An American pilot who used to fly supplies and people regularly to Trox Island. His help is instrumental in aiding Perry Stuart in his effort to find out who owns the island and what is going on there.

Unwin, Bobby (*Whip Hand*). A journalist at the *Daily Planet*. Sid Halley exchanges information with him.

Updike, Mr. and Mrs. Harry (*In the Frame*). Charles Todd and Jik and Sarah Cassavetes visit them in New Zealand to see a suspicious painting they have recently purchased. They warn them that they could be the next robbery victims.

Upjohn, Ronnie (*Comeback*). A racehorse owner, he is threatening to sue Ken McClure for malpractice after the death of one of his horses, which Ken had operated upon.

Upton, Erica (*Longshot*). Harry Goodhaven's aunt, and a famous literary author. She is also famous for her pithy putdowns of aspiring middle-brow writers like John Kendall.

Urquhart, Phil (*Straight*). Veterinarian who assists Derek Franklin in running tests on his brother's horse, Dozen Roses.

Usher, Benjamin, aka Benjy (*Driving Force*). A racehorse owner and trainer who, oddly enough, cannot bear touching horses. He quarrels constantly with his wife Dot.

Usher, Dot (*Driving Force*). Benjy's wife; she is a regular verbal combatant with her husband.

van Dysart, Mrs. (*Odds Against*). She and her husband come to stay with Admiral Roland for the weekend, and she insults Sid Halley constantly. The admiral finds her useful to his plans because "she has a tongue like a rattlesnake."

van Dysart, Rex (*Odds Against*). Admiral Roland invites him and his wife for the weekend as part of his plan to challenge Sid Halley into starting an investigation into the shenanigans going on at Seabury racecourse.

van Els, Jett (*Second Wind*). She is the latest in a series of nurses that have taken care of Perry Stuart's grandmother Mrs. Mevagissey. Perry is immediately attracted to her.

van Huren, Quentin (*Smokescreen*). Nerissa Cavesey's brother-in-law's brother. He owns a gold mine, Rojedda Reef, and takes Link Lincoln and others to visit it, with ominous results. His wife is Vivi, and his children are Jonathan and Sally.

Vaughnley, Hugh (*Break In*). Son of Lord Vaughnley, whose taste for high-stakes gambling causes his father quite a bit of trouble.

Vaughnley, Lady (*Break In*). Wife of newspaper magnate Lord Vaughnley.

Vaughnley, Lord (*Bolt*; *Break In*). Owner of the *Towncrier* newspaper, he is active in the running of his paper, and he is the unwitting target of a conspiracy, from which he can only be extricated by Kit Fielding.

Venables, Patrick (*Driving Force*). The head security man at the Jockey Club. He sends Nina Young out as an undercover agent to help Freddie Croft.

Verity, Gina (*Shattered*). The mother of Victor Waltman Verity and the sister of Rose Payne.

Verity, Victor Waltman (*Shattered*). A teenager, living in Taunton, who contacts Gerard Logan over the Internet with some important news.

Vernon (*Proof*). Liquor manager for the caterers at Martineau Park racecourse, and associate of Paul Young.

Vickers, Gareth (*Longshot*). Tremayne's fifteen-year-old son. He is a schoolboy who can manage well on his own, except in the matter of cooking. He wants John Kendall to teach him about survival techniques.

Vickers, Mackie (*Longshot*). She is married to Perkin Vickers, and she is Tremayne Vickers's assistant in running his stables.

Vickers, Perkin (*Longshot*). Tremayne's older son, who is married to Mackie. He makes beautiful hand-carved and individually designed furniture.

Vickers, Tremayne (*Longshot*). A famous and successful racehorse trainer, he has trained almost a thousand winners in fifty years of racing. He hires John Kendall to stay in his house and write his biography.

Victor (*Dead Cert*). Stable lad who attends to Admiral, Bill Davidson's horse.

Viking, John (*Whip Hand*). A daredevil balloonist who takes Sid Halley up with him during a balloon race.

Villars, Annie (*Rat Race*). A trainer with a sharp tongue. "She can roust her stable lads out on the gallops in words a sergeant-major never thought of. But sweet as milk with the owners . . . She knows what a horse can do and what it can't, and that's most of the battle in this game."

Vincent, Vic (*Knockdown*). Bloodstock agent who can do no wrong in the eyes of his biggest client, Constantine Brevett. Jonah Dereham suspects that he may not have Brevett's best interests at heart.

Vine, George and Poppet (*High Stakes*). Racehorse owners whose trainer is Rupert Ramsey. Felicity Leeds introduces them to crooked bookie Ganser Mays.

Vine, Joanie ("Song for Mona," *Field of Thirteen*). The social-climbing daughter of Mona Watkins, who is ashamed of her working-class mother.

Vine, Peregrine ("Song for Mona," *Field of Thirteen*). Husband of Joanie, assistant to auctioneers of fine art and antiques, he has the type of background his wife esteems.

Vine, Tony (*The Danger*). A colleague of Andrew Douglas's at Liberty Market. Ex-SAS, he is a master at retrieving victims from kidnappers.

Vinichek, Jill (*10 Lb. Penalty*). A Minister of Education whom Ben Juliard meets during a political function.

Visborough, Alison (*Wild Horses*). The daughter of the late Rupert Visborough and his wife Audrey, she is a close friend of Howard Tyler's, and she leaks a story damaging to Thomas Lyon to the press about dissent on the set of his movie. Thomas almost loses his job over this.

Visborough, Audrey (*Wild Horses*). The widow of Rupert Visborough, she is indignant that Thomas Lyon is making a movie about the old scandal involving her late (and mostly unlamented) sister, Sonia, fearing that it will damage her late husband's reputation.

Visborough, Roddy (aka Rodbury) (*Wild Horses*). The seemingly ineffectual brother of Alison and the son of Audrey and the late Rupert Visborough.

Visborough, Rupert (*Wild Horses*). Though he is dead by the time the book opens, he nevertheless has a role to play, since one of the characters in the movie, Cibber, is based on him. It was his wife's sister who was found hanged in the stables in the case which is the basis for the film, and he gave up his political aspirations in the ensuing scandal. His family is dead set against the making of the movie, fearing that it will revile his reputation further.

Vynn, David T. ("Corkscrew," *Field of Thirteen*). A young sharp lawyer, he assists Jules Reginald Harlow in getting to the bottom of a very twisty game.

Wainwright, Commander Lucas (*Whip Hand*). The head of security for the Jockey Club.

Wakefield, Inspector (*Dead Cert*). Policeman present at the West Sussex races to whom Alan York gives a statement about a murderous attack on a fellow jockey.

Wallis, Mr. (*Bonecrack*). Security expert, "all of nineteen," who helps Neil Griffon set up some security at Rowley Lodge stables.

Wally (*For Kicks*). Head lad in the Earl of October's stables.

Wangen, Sven (*Slay-Ride*). Norwegian businessman and racehorse owner; one of the stewards of the Norwegian Jockey Club. Bob Sherman had ridden for him in the past.

Ward, Alexandra (*High Stakes*). She owns a catering business in America and is visiting London when she meets Steven Scott.

Ward, Cassidy Lovelace ("Song for Mona," *Field of Thirteen*). An American and wildly successful country music singer, she is married to Oliver Bolingbroke, and the two of them offer Mona Watkins a job, a home, and a feeling of family.

Warner, Pen (*Banker*). A smart, highly professional pharmacist who is an old friend of Judith and Gordon Michaels. She meets Tim Ekaterin at their house, and brings her specialized knowledge to help find out what is wrong with the foals sired by Sandcastle.

Watermead, Ed (*Driving Force*). The son of Michael and Maudie Watermead, he is "16 and pretty stupid."

Watermead, Maudie (*Driving Force*). She is married to Michael Watermead, a trainer. Her hospitality and sexiness are legendary in the village.

Watermead, Michael (*Driving Force*). A trainer who often has very high-quality horses in his stables.

Watermead, Tessa (*Driving Force*). Michael's seventeen-year-old daughter, she is "full of unspecified resentments."

Watkins, Billy (*Flying Finish*). A groom who works occasionally for Yardman Transport. He hates all aristocrats and takes it out on Henry.

Watkins, Mona ("Song for Mona," *Field of Thirteen*). A Welshwoman who makes her living looking after horses, she isn't quite up to snuff as far as her social-climbing daughter is concerned.

Watson, Bob (*Longshot*). He is the head stable lad at Tremayne Vickers's racing stable.

Watson, Ingrid (*Longshot*). Bob Watson's wife.

Watts, Owen (*Break In*). Employee of the *Daily Flag*, he and his colleague Jay Erskine attempt to dig up dirt on Bobby Allardeck.

Wayfield, Greg (*Comeback*). The American husband of English singer Vicky Larch. Though he has presence, according to Peter Darwin, he doesn't have his wife's stage charisma. Together, they perform a very polished cabaret-style act.

Welfram, Derry (*The Edge*). A rent-a-thug whom Tor Kelsey suspects is working on a blackmail job with Julius Filmer. He dies suddenly at York races.

Wells, Jackson (*Wild Horses*). A trainer whose wife was found hanged in the stables. He is the basis for the character whom Nash Rourke is portraying in the movie based on the case.

Wells, Lucy (*Wild Horses*). The attractive young daughter of Jackson Wells and his second wife. Thomas Lyon, immediately smitten by her, eventually hires her to assist him in cataloging Valentine Clark's library, his legacy from his late friend.

Wells, Mr. (*Risk*). A man with some serious accountancy problems, he proves to be more than a simple problem for Roland Britten's professional skills.

Wells, Oliver (*Decider*). Clerk of the course at Stratton Park. Along with Roger Gardner, he asks Lee Morris for help in saving the racecourse.

Wells, Ridley (*Wild Horses*). The ne'er-do-well brother of Jackson Wells, he is hired briefly by Thomas Lyon to assist with a stunt which, unbeknownst to him, is a recreation of a murderous attack.

Wells, Sonia (*Wild Horses*). The first wife of Jackson Wells, who was found hanged in the stables.

Wells, Tom (*Flying Finish*). Henry Grey flies for him, out of the Fenland Flying Club at a Lincolnshire airport.

Wenkins, Clifford (*Smokescreen*). South African distribution manager for Worldic Cinemas. He tries to get Link Lincoln to do more publicity in order to please his bosses at Worldic, in spite of Link's clear instructions to the contrary.

Wessex, Duke of (*Rat Race*). A racehorse owner. He is vastly kind and a bit dim. His nephew Matthew is his friend and heir.

West, Norman (*Hot Money*). A private investigator, he has worked for Malcolm Pembroke in the past, as well as for another member of the family or two. Malcolm and Ian Pembroke employ him to verify the whereabouts of family members during the attempts on Malcolm's life.

Westering, Sir Ivan (*To the Hilt*). He is Alexander Kinloch's stepfather. He is the owner and CEO of the King Alfred Brewery, which is in serious financial difficulties.

Westering, Vivienne (*To the Hilt*). Alexander Kinloch's mother. She asks for his help when her husband, Sir Ivan, has a heart attack.

Westerland, Sir William ("The Day of the Losers," *Field of Thirteen*). Senior steward of the Jockey Club, to whom the chief superintendent relays the news of suspicious banknotes being passed at Aintree. He's asked to do something unthinkable to help locate the person who passed the note.

Wexford, Ivor (*In the Frame*). The manager of the Yarra River Fine Arts Gallery in Melbourne.

White, Lady Wendy (*Reflex*). Wife of the philandering steward of the Jockey Club and an old schoolmate of Marie Millace.

White, Lord John (*Reflex*). Steward of the Jockey Club, whose infatuation with Dana den Relgan allows Ivor den Relgan to force his way into the Jockey Club.

Wichelsea, Ray ("Corkscrew," *Field of Thirteen*). Owner of the bloodstock agency for whom Sandy Nutbridge works.

Wilcox, Tricksy ("Raid at Kingdom Hill," *Field of Thirteen*). Unemployed punter who finds a new way to make money at Kingdom Hill Racecourse, until fate intervenes.

Wilkerson, Quintus L., III (*Blood Sport*). Hearty fellow guest ("Call me Wilkie") of Gene Hawkins's at the Clives's guest ranch in Wyoming, along with his wife, Betty-Ann, and children, Samantha and Mickey.

Will (*Second Wind*). A weatherman at the Hurricane Center in Miami. Perry Stuart works with him and asks him for some help in tracking down the owners of Trox Island.

Williams, Absalom Elvis da Vinci, aka Bill ("Collision Course," *Field of Thirteen*). Enterprising young newspaper editor, recently sacked from the *Cotswold Voice*, who uses the power of the press to avenge a slight.

Williams, Clarissa (*Straight*). The wife of Lord Knightwood, she is Greville Franklin's mistress. Predictably, she is devastated by Greville's death, but despite her grief she proves to be quick-acting and resilient when Derek Franklin needs her most.

Williams, Henry, Lord Knightwood (*Straight*). The elderly husband of Clarissa Williams, he seems not to suspect that his wife has been having an affair.

Wilson, Jud (*For Kicks*). Head traveling lad in the stables of Hedley Humber.

Worthington (*Shattered*). Chauffeur to Marigold Knight, he also helps Gerard Logan with his investigation into the theft of his money and videotape.

Wright (*Dead Cert*). Subordinate of Inspector Lodge in Maidenhead CID.

Wyfold, Chief Inspector (*Banker*). He is in charge of a particularly nasty murder investigation.

Wyvern, Alderney L. (*10 Lb. Penalty*). A political string-puller, he had been Dennis Nagle's best friend and chief advisor. He is thwarted in his attempts to get Orinda Nagle named her husband's successor as candidate for the election, and he works behind the scenes to derail George Juliard's campaign.

Yale, Detective Superintendent (*Hot Money*). Policeman in charge of the case when Malcolm Pembroke's house, Quantum, is bombed.

Yardley, Alistair (*Risk*). One of a group of young men who seem to wander foreign ports in search of other men's boats to caretake, while their owners go about their business elsewhere.

Yarrow, Wilson (*Decider*). He is Conrad Stratton's tame architect, who produces a set of very unusual plans for rebuilding the seating area for racegoers. Yarrow went to the same architecture school as Lee Morris.

Yates, Dave (*Driving Force*). One of the drivers for Freddie Croft's horse transport business. Dave and another driver pick up a hitchhiker one night and are dismayed to find that he has died along the way. Dave is "primarily a horseman and secondarily a driver."

Yaxley, Elgin (*Reflex*). Owner of racehorses embroiled in a nasty scandal when five of his prize horses were shot to death. Though he could not be officially linked with the crime, he was forced to depart England for a time.

Yeager, Sam (*Longshot*). Chief jockey for Tremayne Vickers. A ladies' man and owner of a boat kept in a decrepit boatyard.

York, Alan (*Dead Cert*). The hero. Twenty-four and reared in Southern Rhodesia, he is an amateur jockey who works several days a week in the London office of his father's trading company. He has lived with the Davidson family for seven months.

York, Mr. (*Dead Cert*). Alan York's wealthy businessman father. He comes to check on Alan's welfare after Alan has a bad fall at the Bristol races, in a fashion similar to the accident that killed Bill Davidson.

Yorkshire, Owen Cliff (*Come to Grief*). He is chief shareholder and managing director of a horse nut (horse feed) company called Topline Foods.

Young, Chris (*To the Hilt*). A private eye and bodyguard to Alexander Kinloch; a man who has a way with disguises.

Young, Courtney (*10 Lb. Penalty*). Racehorse owner whose horse is killed in an accident during a race at Taunton. She tearfully confesses to Ben Juliard that she has no insurance on her horse, and from this Ben gets the idea, eventually, to work for the company, Weatherbys, who are the premier firm in insuring racehorses.

Young, Cumber and Rose (*The Edge*). A married couple who own the racehorse Sparrowgrass and are traveling on the race train across Canada.

Young, Nina (*Driving Force*). An undercover investigator sent to Freddie

Croft's by the Jockey Club. Although she is older than Freddie, she still fascinates him emotionally and sexually. "She was lonely, I perceived, surprised, the hard outer lady a gallant way of playing the cards life had dealt her."

Young, Paddy (*Whip Hand*). The head lad at George Caspar's training stables.

Young, Paul (*Proof*). He says that he's from the head office of the owners of the Silver Moondance Restaurant, but Tony Beach has reason to doubt him.

Young, Ursula (*Banker*). A bloodstock agent who gives good advice to Tim Ekaterin.

Young, Vic (*Bonecrack*). Traveling head lad and assistant to Etty Craig at Rowley Lodge stables.

Young, Wilton (*Knockdown*). A deadly rival of Constantine Brevett's, he is one of Jonah Dereham's chief suspects as he attempts to uncover the full truth of the kickback scheme.

Zarac (*Proof*). The wine waiter at the Silver Moondance Restaurant; he is murdered in a particularly brutal way.

Zeissen, Paul M. (*Blood Sport*). An official of the Buttress Life Insurance company, which had insurance on Dave Teller's missing racehorses.

A DICK FRANCIS GAZETTEER

Dick Francis has set novels in locations all over the world. Wherever the books take place, however, one thing is consistently true: the settings are authentic. In many cases, Dick and Mary Francis traveled extensively as part of the research for the books. In the case of *Blood Sport*, for example, they took Greyhound buses all over the United States in the 1960s, researching locations for the book. They've been to Africa, Russia, Norway, Canada, and Australia to do research for other novels.

If Dick Francis has a favorite location, however, it must be Berkshire. Many books have scenes set in the open country west of London and south of Oxford, where strings of horses are exercised on the Downs and the small village of Lambourn holds many a racing stable. Dick and Mary Francis built a house in Berkshire, near the village of Blewbury, and lived in it for many years. This is their heartland.

Ascot racecourse. Gene Hawkins goes to the races in *Blood Sport*; Rob Finn rides here in *Nerve*; Tim Ekaterin goes to the races and sees Sandcastle here for the first time in *Banker*; Kit Fielding rides here in *Break*

In; the Millace family lives near here in *Reflex*; Jonah Dereham in *Knockdown* tries to buy a horse for Mrs. Kerry Sanders at Ascot sales and then is menaced by thugs who want the horse.

Australia. Charles Todd investigates art fraud here in *In the Frame*. He meets Jik and Sarah Cassavetes in Sydney; they travel together to Melbourne for Melbourne Cup Day, then go on to Alice Springs. Daniel Roke is a successful young stud farm owner in Australia in *For Kicks*, when he is approached to take on a tricky undercover assignment. Malcolm and Ian Pembroke go to the Melbourne Cup in *Hot Money*.

Bedfordshire. Henry Grey's family home is here in *Flying Finish*.

Berkshire. Kelly Hughes lives in the county in *Enquiry*; Link lives in a village "far up the Thames" and rides on the Berkshire Downs in *Smokescreen*; Gordon and Ginnie Quint live here in *Come to Grief*; Jack Hawthorn's stable is in the Downs, and Tony Beach lives in a "small Thames-side town" in *Proof*; the Pembroke family home, Quantum, is here in *Hot Money*; and Alexander Kinloch rides Golden Malt out on the Downs in *To the Hilt*.

Birmingham. Crooked private eye David Oakley lives here, and Rob Finn goes here to find out about him in *Enquiry*.

Bologna, Italy. The Cenci family live here in *The Danger*.

Bracknell. Serena Pembroke lives in this Berkshire town in *Hot Money*.

Brighton. The gang of violent taxi drivers in *Dead Cert* is from Brighton.

George Juliard meets his son Ben here, and asks him to help him in his parliamentary campaign in *10 Lb. Penalty*.

Brighton racecourse. Alessia Cenci and Andrew Douglas go to Brighton races in *The Danger*.

Bristol. Gerard Logan goes to Bristol to meet with George Lawson-Young and see his laboratory in *Shattered*.

Bristol racecourse. Alan York in *Dead Cert* rides a race at this fictional racecourse.

Broadway. Gerard Logan has his glass shop at home in this small, touristy Cotswold village in *Shattered*.

Buckingham. Derrydown Sky Taxis is headquartered near here in *Rat Race*.

Buenos Aires. Henry Grey flies here with racehorses in *Flying Finish*.

Burgess Hill, Sussex. Kate Ellery-Penn lives near here in *Dead Cert*.

Cambridge. The Ross family lives in Newmarket near here in *Rat Race*, and Matt Shore flies in and out of the airport, while it's during Nancy Ross's first solo flight from Haydock racecourse to Cambridge that her electrical system goes out and Matt must save her. Malcolm Pembroke holes up here while fleeing from his grasping family in *Hot Money*.

Canada. Most of *The Edge* is set on the Great Transcontinental Mystery

Racing Train going across Canada from Ottawa to Vancouver, with stops in Toronto and Winnipeg.

Canterbury. Rachel Ferns is in the hospital here in *Come to Grief*.

The Caribbean. In *Second Wind*, Perry Stuart and Kris Ironside fly to Grand Cayman Island in the Caribbean to pick up Robin Darcy's small plane. They fly to Trox Island, then through the eye of Hurricane Odin over the sea.

Cheltenham. When Rob Finn in *Nerve* gets a job with the Axminster stable, he moves to a village near Cheltenham, while much of the action in *Comeback* takes place in and around Cheltenham.

Cheltenham racecourse. Most of Dick Francis's jockeys seem to race at Cheltenham, including Alan York in *Dead Cert*; Rob Finn in *Nerve*; Henry Grey in *Flying Finish*; Roland Britten in *Risk*; and Kit Fielding in *Break In*. Malcolm and Ian Pembroke go here in *Hot Money*, and Ian rides Park Railings; Jonah Dereham comes here in *Knockdown*; and Martin Stukely dies in a fall here in *Shattered*.

> *I stopped for a while on Cleeve Hill, overlooking Cheltenham race-course, seeing below me the white rails, the green grass, the up-and-downhill supreme test for steeplechasers. The Grand National was a great exciting lottery, but the Cheltenham Gold Cup sorted out the true enduring stars.* Comeback

Chichester. Andrew Douglas and Alessia Cenci go to the police station in Chichester when Dominic Nerrity is kidnapped near here in *The Danger*.

Chiswick, London. Danielle de Brescou's office is here in *Break In* and *Bolt*; John Kendall lives here in a freezing garret at the beginning of *Longshot*.

Cirencester. Antonia Huntercombe lives in Paley, near Cirencester, in *Knockdown*.

City of London. The Paul Ekaterin Bank is in the City, near St. Paul's, in *Banker*.

Clapham Common. Judith and Gordon Michael live here in *Banker*.

Combe Bassett. In *Come to Grief*, Betty Bracken lives in this village that is south of Hungerford in Berkshire.

Cookham, Berkshire. Ian Pembroke stays in a pub here after his father's house is bombed in *Hot Money*.

Corrie, Berkshire. This fictional town is where Kelly Hughes lives in *Enquiry*.

The Cotswolds. Bill and Scilla Davidson have a house in the Cotswolds in *Dead Cert*; the jockey Peter Cloony lives in a Cotswolds village near Cheltenham in *Nerve*; Nerissa Cavesey lives here in *Smokescreen*.

Dalwhinnie, Scotland. In *To the Hilt*, Alexander Kinloch meets Jed Parlane here, and gets on the train at the station to go to London.

Devon and Exeter racecourse. Kit Fielding rides here in *Break In*.

Didcot. In *Longshot*, John Kendall does the shopping here for the Vickers household.

Doncaster racecourse. Tim meets bloodstock agent Ursula Young here for the first time in *Banker*; Jonah Dereham goes to Doncaster races and sales in *Knockdown*.

Dorset. In *10 Lb. Penalty*, the Hoopwestern constituency that George Juliard is contesting is in Dorset.

Dunstable racecourse. *Nerve* opens at the fictional Dunstable races.

Edinburgh. In *Driving Force*, Freddie Croft goes to Edinburgh to see his sister Lizzie and deliver samples to a scientist at the university.

Epsom. Jonah Dereham goes to Vic Vincent's house in a crucial scene in *Knockdown*; Ian Pembroke lives here in a "rather dull suburban flat" in *Hot Money*.

Epsom Downs racecourse. Sid Halley goes to the Derby in *Come to Grief*.

Exeter. Ben Juliard goes to university here in *Hot Money*.

Exmoor. Gerard Logan, Victor Verity, and Tom Pigeon have a peaceful day out on Exmoor in *Shattered*.

Frodsham. A town in Cheshire where Topline Foods is headquartered in *Come to Grief*.

Hampstead. Neil Griffon has a flat here in *Bonecrack*, and his lover Gillie is also his lodger.

Haydock racecourse. In *Rat Race*, Matt Shore flies Colin Ross and other passengers to Haydock in an air taxi.

Heathbury Park racecourse. This fictional racecourse is featured in *Forfeit*.

Heathrow. Charles Todd lives in a "noisy flat near Heathrow Airport" in *In the Frame*.

Henley. The boating trip on the Thames that Simon Keeble arranges for Gene Hawkins leaves from Henley in *Blood Sport*; in *Hot Money*, Donald and Helen Pembroke live here, and he manages the golf club.

Hereford racecourse. Rob Finn in *Nerve* rides here.

Hertfordshire. In *Banker*, Oliver Knowles's stud farm is in this county.

High Wycombe. Ginnie Knowles goes to school here in *Banker*.

Hitchen. In *Break In*, Major and Mrs. Perryside live here in poverty after encountering Maynard Allardeck at his worst.

Hoopwestern. The fictional seat for which George Juliard stands in his bid to be elected to parliament in *10 Lb. Penalty*.

Hungerford. Derek Franklin lives here in *Straight*; Oliver Grantchester lives near here in *To the Hilt*.

Ipswich. Greville Franklin is killed in an accident here at the opening of *Straight*.

Isle of Wight. In *Risk*, Roland Britten and Jossie Finch go to the Isle of

Wight for a day out; Roland grew up on the island and he shows her the sights.

Itchenor. Three-year-old Dominic Nerrity is held in a house here by kidnappers in *The Danger*.

Johannesburg, South Africa. Link Lincoln flies here to check on Nerissa Cavesey's racehorses in *Smokescreen*.

Kempton Park racecourse. In *Dead Cert*, Alan York rides a race here. Roland Britten rides here in *Risk*, as do Ian Pembroke in *Hot Money*, and Henry Grey in *Flying Finish*.

Kensington, London. In *Nerve*, Rob Finn's family flat is in Kensington, two or three streets back from Hyde Park; Ronnie Curzon's office, where John Kendall first meets Tremayne Vickers, is here in *Longshot*; Andrew Douglas lives in Kensington near his office in *The Danger*.

Kent. Linda and Rachel Ferns live in the county in *Come to Grief*.

Kingdom Hill. Fictional racecourse that is the principal setting for the story "Raid at Kingdom Hill" in the short-story collection *Field of Thirteen*.

Kingman, Arizona. Matt Clive is holed up at a ranch here in *Blood Sport*.

Kruger National Park, South Africa. Link Lincoln and others go to see the wildlife in the park, with dire results, in *Smokescreen*.

Lambourn. One of the two main racing locations in Francis novels, along with Newmarket. The area near Lambourn in Berkshire is also perhaps the most heavily used location in the books. The Cranfields have their training stable near Lambourn in *Enquiry*; Popsy Teddington has her training stables here in *The Danger*; Kit Fielding lives here in *Break In*, as does Philip Nore in *Reflex*; Ian Pembroke moves here in *Hot Money*; Emily Cox, Alexander Kinloch's wife, has her training stables here in *To the Hilt*.

> *Golden Malt thought he knew where he was going, which helped at first but not later. He tossed his head with pleasure and trotted jauntily up the rutted access to the downlands which spread for fifty miles east to west across central southern England—from the Chiltern Hills to Salisbury Plain. I felt more at home on the Downs than in Lambourn itself, but even there solitude was rare: strings of horses cluttered every skyline and trainers' Land-Rovers bumped busily in their wake. Lambourn's industry lay out there on the sweeping green uplands in the wind and the prehistoric mornings.*   To the Hilt

Las Vegas. Gene Hawkins's investigation in *Blood Sport* takes him here briefly.

Laurel racecourse. The festive international race is run at this course near Washington, D.C., in *The Danger*.

Leicester racecourse. Worthington the chauffeur and Gerard Logan go to the races together in *Shattered*.

Lexington, Kentucky. Gene Hawkins investigates the missing racehorses here in *Blood Sport*; in *Hot Money*, Malcolm Pembroke comes here to look at bloodstock.

Lincolnshire. In *Flying Finish*, Henry Grey flies small planes from the Fenland Flying Club in Lincolnshire.

Liverpool. Sid Halley was born and grew up in the Liverpool slums.

London. Hunt Radnor Associates is located on the Cromwell Road in *Odds Against*; Yardman Transport, where Henry Grey works in *Flying Finish*, is on a Thames-side wharf in the Pool of London; Gene Hawkins lives in Putney, and Lynnie Keeble stays in a hostel in South Kensington in *Blood Sport*; the Jockey Club is headquartered in Portman Square; Steven Scott lives at Regents Park Malthouse in *High Stakes*; Roland stays at the Gloucester Hotel in *Risk*; the Liberty Market firm is headquartered here in *The Danger*; Tor Kelsey lives in Kennington near the Oval cricket grounds in *The Edge*; David Cleveland lives "behind the Brompton Road" in *Slay-Ride*; George Juliard goes to Westminster and lives at Canary Wharf in *10 Lb. Penalty*; Perry Stuart and Kris Ironside work at the BBC Weather Centre in *Second Wind*; the Princess Casilia, Roland and Danielle de Brescou live in Eaton Square, and much of the action in *Bolt* takes place in London, as Kit Fielding tries to neutralize the thug threatening them; Derek Franklin in *Straight* spends much of his time in London, trying to sort out the aftermath of his brother's death; Ty Tyrone in *Forfeit* works on Fleet Street; Sid Halley lives in Pont Square off Cadogan Square in *Come to Grief*; Sir Ivan and Lady Westering live at Park Crescent near Regent's Park in *To the Hilt*; Ian and Malcolm Pembroke stay at the Savoy and later the Ritz in *Hot Money*; Saxony Franklin is in Hatton Garden in *Straight*.

Longchamp racecourse. In *Hot Money*, Ian and Malcolm Pembroke go to see Malcolm's new horse, Blue Clancy, race in the Arc de Triomphe at this racecourse near Paris.

Los Angeles. Malcolm and Ian Pembroke go to see the Breeders' Cup race at Santa Anita racecourse in *Hot Money*.

Louisville, Kentucky. The site of the Kentucky Derby, and the setting for the story "The Gift" in the collection *Field of Thirteen*.

Lynton. Dr. Adam Force lives in this Devonshire town in *Shattered*.

Maidenhead. Sam's boat and boathouse are here in *Longshot*; Gervase Pembroke lives here in *Hot Money*.

Maidenhead racecourse. The opening scene in *Dead Cert* and some other scenes in the book are set at this fictional racecourse.

Marlow. Lucy and Edwin Pembroke live in this Berkshire town in *Hot Money*.

Martineau Park racecourse. A climactic scene in *Proof* takes place at this fictional racecourse located near Oxford.

Miami. Steven Scott visits Alexandra Ward at her cousin's house here, and they go to the Hialeah Thoroughbred sales in *High Stakes*; the opening scenes of *Comeback* are set here.

Milan, Italy. Gabriella Barzini in *Flying Finish* works at the gift shop at Malpensa Airport in Milan, and Henry Grey meets her there while he's accompanying horses to Italy.

Minorca. In *Risk*, Roland Britten is kidnapped and kept on a sailboat; he escapes from it in Minorca.

Monadhliath Mountains. A mountain range between Loch Ness and Aviemore in Scotland. Alexander Kinloch's cottage is here in *To the Hilt*.

Moscow. Most of the action in *Trial Run* takes place here.

Newbury. Colin Ross races here in *Rat Race*, as do Kit Fielding in *Break In*, and Henry Grey in *Flying Finish*. Roland Britten is junior partner in an accountancy firm in Newbury in *Risk*; Bob and Emma Sherman live near Newbury in *Slay-Ride*.

Newmarket. Newmarket is the headquarters of British racing. Many Francis novels have scenes set here; perhaps the most atmospheric is *Bonecrack*, where Neil Griffon takes over management of his father's training stables, called Rowley Lodge. George and Rosemary Caspar have their stables here in *Whip Hand*; Calder Jackson's healing establishment is here in *Banker*; Holly and Bobby Allardeck live here in *Break In*; Ian meets his father at Newmarket sales for the first time in three years in *Hot Money*; Thomas Lyon is filming in and around here in *Wild Horses*; Jonah Dereham goes to Newmarket sales and races in *Knockdown*.

New York City. In *Flying Finish*, Henry Grey flies here, and it's on the return trip to London that he must kill a horse whose panic is endangering the airplane. Gene Hawkins in *Blood Sport* travels to New York to meet with Walt Prensela at the Buttress Life Insurance offices on Thirty-third Street; Ian Pembroke spends a few days in the city while waiting to meet his father in *Hot Money*.

New Zealand. Charles Todd and Jik and Sarah Cassavetes travel here to visit other victims of art fraud in *In the Frame*. They fly to Auckland, then drive to Wellington, where a climactic and violent scene takes place.

North London. Neil Griffon's father is in hospital here in *Bonecrack*; Kenneth Charter's transport firm is here in *Proof*.

Norway. Most of the action in *Slay-Ride* takes place in Norway.

Norwich. Some key scenes in *Twice Shy* are set here.

Nottingham. In *Rat Race*, Matt Shore diverts his air taxi to East Midlands Airport near here when he thinks something is wrong with it; shortly after the passengers disembark, the plane blows up. Tor Kelsey goes to the races at Nottingham in *The Edge*.

Oxford. Jenny Halley and Louise McInnes share a flat here in *Whip Hand*.

Oxfordshire. Admiral Roland's rambling old house, Aynsford, is in Oxfordshire, and Sid Halley finds refuge in it in *Odds Against, Whip Hand*, and *Come to Grief*.

Paris. Henry Grey flies here in a cargo plane with horses in *Flying Finish*; Sid Halley holes up here for a few days after he's threatened in *Whip Hand*.

Pixhill. The fictional village on the Berkshire Downs where Freddie Croft lives and has his transport business in *Driving Force*.

Plumpton racecourse. Alan York races here in *Dead Cert*, as does Kit Fielding in *Break In*; Charles Todd goes to the races and meets Maisie Mathews here in *In the Frame*; David Cleveland goes to the races here in *Slay-Ride*.

Reading. Dave Teller, in *Blood Sport*, is in the hospital here; the Silver Moondance Restaurant is near Reading in *Proof*; Ellis Quint is on trial at Reading Law Courts in *Come to Grief*; the offices of the accountants and Margaret Morden are here in *To the Hilt*; Mackie Vickers and others meet John Kendall at the train station here in *Longshot*.

Redcar racecourse. Matt Shore flies clients to the races here in *Rat Race*; he meets the Duke of Wessex and his nephew Matthew, and saves the jockey Kenny Bayst from a savage beating.

St. Albans. Philip Nore's grandmother is in a nursing home here in *Reflex*.

Sandown Park racecourse. Many Dick Francis heroes ride in races here, including Rob Finn in *Nerve*, Henry Grey in *Flying Finish*, Kit Fielding in *Bolt*, and Ian Pembroke in *Hot Money*. Steven Scott confronts Jody Leeds about his theft here in *High Stakes*; John Kendall goes to the races with Mackie Vickers in *Longshot*; and the opening scene of *Reflex* is set here.

> *Sandown racecourse, right-handed, undulating, with seven fences close together down the far side, was a track where good jumpers could excel. I particularly liked riding there, and it was a good place for Abseil, except that the uphill finish could find him out. To win there, he had to be flying in the lead coming round the last long bend, and jump the last three fences at his fastest speed. Then, if he faded on the hill, one might just hang on in front as far as the post.* Bolt

Santa Barbara, California. Part of the action of *Blood Sport* is set here, as Gene Hawkins tracks down the missing racehorses.

Seabury racecourse. The fictional Seabury is the racecourse that Sid Halley tries to save in *Odds Against*.

Shellerton. The Vickers household, in *Longshot*, lives in this fictional village near Reading.

Shelley Green. A village in Berkshire where Archie Kirk lives in *Come to Grief*.

Shropshire. Donald and Regina Stuart's house, which is burgled to such fatal effect, is here in *In the Frame*.

Six Mile Bottom. Trainer William Derry lives in this village near Newmarket in *Twice Shy*.

South Africa. Much of the action of *Smokescreen* takes place here.

Southampton. In *Driving Force*, Freddie Croft is thrown unconscious into the sea near Southampton Docks.

South Mimms. Two of Freddie Croft's horse van drivers, Brett Gardner and Dave Yates, pick up a hitchhiker at the South Mimms service station in North London in *Driving Force*. They find the hitchhiker dead in their van the next time they stop.

Spain. The film *Man in a Car*, with Edward Lincoln, is being filmed in southern Spain in *Smokescreen*.

Stratford-on-Avon racecourse. Steven Scott goes here with Energise's substitute in *High Stakes*.

Surrey. Hilary Pinlock lives in Surrey in *Risk*; Lee Morris lives on the Surrey-Sussex border in *Decider*; the Nerritys live in Surrey near Epsom in *The Danger*; Jonah Dereham in *Knockdown* lives in Surrey, five miles down the road from Gatwick Airport, while Sophie Randolph lives in Esher, Surrey.

Sussex. In *High Stakes*, the trainer Rupert Ramsey takes Steven's horse Energise into his stables in Sussex.

Swindon. In *Decider*, the fictional Stratton Park racecourse is located near Swindon.

Taunton. In *Shattered*, the Verity family (Gina and her son Victor) live in a terrace house in Taunton.

Thames River. In the story "Collision Course" in the collection *Field of Thirteen*, journalist Bill Williams travels by boat down the river and has an encounter at a riverside restaurant that has interesting repercussions.

Toronto. Merry & Co., the travel agents who organize the mystery race train, are headquartered in Toronto in *The Edge*.

Towcester racecourse. In *Risk*, Roland rides here, as does Kit in *Break In*.

> *Towcester was a deep-country course, all rolling green hills sixty*
> *miles to the north-west of London.* Break In

Tunbridge Wells. Peter Rammileese has a house and indoor riding arena here in *Whip Hand*.

Twickenham. Jonathan Derry lives here in *Twice Shy*.

Vancouver, Canada. The last stop for the mystery race train in *The Edge*.

Wantage. In *To the Hilt*, the King Alfred Brewery is headquartered at Wantage.

Warwick. The Racegoers' Accident Fund is headquartered here in *Rat Race*.

Warwick racecourse. Matt Shore in *Rat Race* goes to the races; Rob Finn rides here in *Nerve*.

Washington, D.C. Alessia Cenci and Andrew Douglas are both staying here when the last kidnapping occurs in *The Danger*.

Wellingborough. The racing insurance firm of Weatherbys, where Ben Juliard goes to work, is located here in *10 Lb. Penalty*.

Welwyn Garden City. In *Twice Shy*, Angelo Gilbert lives here.

West Wittering. Dominic Nerrity is kidnapped from the beach in this seaside town in *The Danger*.

Wetherby racecourse. In *Flying Finish*, Henry Grey races here.

White Waltham. *Rat Race* starts with an air taxi trip from here to Newbury and onward to Haydock racecourse; Kris Ironside keeps his plane here in *Second Wind*.

Wincanton racecourse. Ben Juliard wins his first race on Sarah's Future here in *10 Lb. Penalty*.

Winchester racecourse. The fictional setting for the story "Haig's Death" in the collection *Field of Thirteen*.

Windsor racecourse. John Kendall goes to the races when Tremayne Vickers has runners here in *Longshot*.

Winnipeg, Canada. Winnipeg is one of the stops for the mystery race train in *The Edge*.

Wokingham, Berkshire. Ferdinand and Debs Pembroke live here in *Hot Money*.

Worthing. Maisie Matthews lives in her beloved house, Treasure Holme, here in *In the Frame*.

Wyoming. Gene Hawkins stays at a dude ranch here in *Blood Sport*.

York races. Derek Franklin watches Dozen Roses race and meets Clarissa Williams and her husband here in *Straight; The Edge* opens at York races, where Tor Kelsey is following a dubious associate of Julius Apollo Filmer.

RACING LINKS

Here are links to some web sites that feature (and explain) British racing and racecourses.

Cheltenham Racecourse
http://www.cheltenham.co.uk

Come Racing
http://www.comeracing.co.uk

Britain's 59 Racecourses
http://www.comeracing.co.uk/courses.htm

The Jockey Club (This site even has reports and results of official enquiries like the one described in *Enquiry*!)
http://www.thejockeyclub.co.uk

British Racing News
http://www.britishracingnews.com

"BIG HORSES OVER BIG FENCES": HORSES FEATURED IN DICK FRANCIS'S BOOKS

Although not all Dick Francis books are primarily about horse racing, horses tend to be central to his works. We pay tribute here to the memorable horses of many novels.

> *Beautiful, marvelous creatures whose responses and instincts worked on a plane as different from humans' as water and oil, not mingling even where they touched. Insight into their senses and consciousness had been like an opening door, a foreign language glimpsed and half learned, full comprehension maddeningly balked by not having the right sort of hearing or sense of smell, nor sufficient skill in telepathy. The feeling of oneness with horses I'd sometimes had in the heat of a race had been their gift to an inferior being; and maybe my passion for winning had been my gift to them. The urge to get to the front was born in them; all they needed was to be shown where and when to go. It could fairly be said that like most jump jockeys, I had aided and abetted horses beyond the bounds of common sense.*
>
> *Whip Hand*

This index is not a comprehensive listing of every horse mentioned in the novels. Rather than include the over three hundred horses mentioned in the novels, we have limited the names here to those who play a more direct role in the plots of the books.

Admiral (*Dead Cert*). The gallant champion Major Bill Davidson is riding when he has a fatal accident; later Admiral carries Alan York to safety on a thrilling cross-country ride.

Allyx (*Blood Sport*). One of the missing racehorses Gene Hawkins is seeking.

Archangel (*Bonecrack*). The favorite to win the Derby; Enso Rivera insists that his son be able to ride this champion, or else.

Bernina (*Break In*). Owned by the Princess Casilia de Brescou. "Bernina, named after the mountain to the south of St. Moritz, had by four years old produced none of the grandeur of the Alps, and to my mind was never going to."

Bethesda (*Whip Hand*). Formerly a racehorse trained by George Caspar, she dies while foaling.

Billyboy ("Spring Fever," *Field of Thirteen*). Horse belonging to Mrs. Angela Hart.

Black Fire (*High Stakes*). A racehorse, bought by Steven Scott in Miami, who looks very much like his horse Energise.

Blue Clancy (*Hot Money*). As part of his newly minted interest in racing,

Malcolm Pembroke buys a half share of this hot favorite, and watches him race in Washington, D.C., and Australia.

Brunelleschi (*The Danger*). A great Italian racehorse, often ridden by Alessia Cenci. He is entered in the International race at Laurel racecourse near Washington, D.C. and is part of the final climactic events of the novel.

Bubbleglass (*High Stakes*). A racehorse owned by Steven Scott.

Buttonhook (*Nerve*). A calm brown mare that Rob Finn buys in order to carry out his scheme of revenge against the villain who has tried to destroy his career.

Cascade (*Bolt*). One of the Princess Casilia de Brescou's horses that is murdered.

Charcoal (*For Kicks*). One of the horses suspected of having been doped in the ongoing scheme.

Chickweed (*Longshot*). The murdered stable lad, Angela Brickell, supposedly gave him chocolate to eat before a race, which is considered doping by racecourse authorities.

Chin-Chin (*For Kicks*). One of the horses owned by Hedley Humber.

Chink (*Smokescreen*). One of Nerissa Cavesey's South African horses, which Link Lincoln goes to see perform at the races.

Chrysalis (*Blood Sport*). One of the missing racehorses Gene Hawkins is seeking.

Chrysos (*Hot Money*). A promising yearling.

Claypits ("Raid at Kingdom Hill," *Field of Thirteen*). The horse that Tricksy Wilcox decides isn't worth a bet.

Col (*Bolt*). One of the Princess Casilia de Brescou's horses that is murdered.

Cotopaxi (*Bolt*). One of the Princess Casilia de Brescou's horses that is murdered.

Crinkle Cut ("The Gift," *Field of Thirteen*). Somerset Farms' entry in the Kentucky Derby, to be ridden by Piper Boles, a jockey not averse to manipulating a race, if the price is right.

Darling Boy ("Blind Chance," *Field of Thirteen*). One of the finishers in a contested race at Ascot.

Daylight (*Reflex*). A horse belonging to Victor Briggs, who wants Philip Nore to lose the race he's riding at Sandown Park racecourse. Philip has lost races before at Briggs's request, but he's beginning to chafe at doing so.

Dial (*High Stakes*). A novice racehorse owned by Steven Scott.

Dobbin (*For Kicks*). One of the horses involved, Daniel Roke suspects, in the doping scheme he's investigating.

Dozen Roses (*Straight*). A racehorse owned by Greville Franklin, he was gelded without his owner's permission by the trainer, Nicholas Loder, and Derek Franklin suspects that the horse might have been drugged in some fashion. Loder wants to buy the horse from Derek, but Derek obstinately refuses, which leads to difficulties.

Drifter (*Longshot*). A nine-year-old gelding. John Kendall is promoted to ride him after he does well on his first mount in Tremayne Vickers's stables.

Energise (*High Stakes*). A racehorse owned by Steven Scott. He has great potential, but unfortunately his trainer, Jody Leeds, is a crook. Jody goes to great lengths to keep Energise, even after he and Steven have fallen out, thus arousing Steven's curiosity and determination. Energise is the first horse that Steven has spent much time with and gotten to know well, and this knowledge is crucial to the plot.

Fable ("Haig's Death," *Field of Thirteen*). Horse that has the potential to change the fortunes of two brothers, Vernon and Villiers Arkwright.

Ferryboat (*High Stakes*). A promising colt owned by Steven Scott. Unfortunately, after being trained for a while by Jody Leeds, Ferryboat doesn't seem to like racing anymore.

Flokati (*The Edge*). A horse traveling on the race train. Flokati is due to race at Winnipeg.

Flotilla (*Whip Hand*). A Derby favorite trained by Martin England, an old friend of Sid Halley's. Martin asks Sid to ride him at the gallops, and Sid's unexpected success at doing so, even with only one hand, helps to restore his sense of self-respect and courage.

Forlorn Hope (*Dead Cert*). Five-year-old brown gelding recently acquired by Alan York to be trained for steeplechase racing.

Fringe (*Longshot*). After successfully riding Touchy and Drifter, John Kendall gets to work on the gallops on Fringe, who is "younger, whippier and less predictable than Drifter."

Gleaner (*Whip Hand*). A heavily favored racehorse who unexpectedly loses a big race due to a previously undetected heart murmur. He is put out to stud, and his problems there provide Sid Halley with crucial information for his investigation.

Golden Malt (*To the Hilt*). A champion racehorse owned by Sir Ivan Westering. He often represents the King Alfred Brewery, and the brewery's creditors may think he is an asset that should be sold as part of the bankruptcy proceedings. Sir Ivan asks Alexander Kinloch to hide him; Alexander's job is complicated by the fact that the horse is being trained by his estranged wife Emily Cox. In a memorable scene, Alexander rides the horse on the Berkshire Downs at night.

Hamlet ("Spring Fever," *Field of Thirteen*). One of the horses owned by Mrs. Angela Hart.

"Harvey's filly" (*Second Wind*). A promising filly trained by Caspar Harvey, she is found in her stall one day, banging her head repeatedly against the wall. She becomes very ill, and radiation poisoning is suspected, but nobody can figure out how it could possibly have happened.

Haunted House ("The Day of the Losers," *Field of Thirteen*). The horse Jerry Springwood is riding in the Grand National at Aintree.

Hearse Puller (*Knockdown*). When Jonah Dereham attempts to buy this horse for Mrs. Kerry Sanders, he gets a nasty surprise.

Heavens Above (*Dead Cert*). Chestnut horse belonging to Kate Ellery-Penn. Alan York is engaged to ride the horse in the Amateur 'Chase.

Hermes (*High Stakes*). A racehorse owned by Steven Scott.

Indian Silk (*Banker*). A racehorse owned by Ricky Barnet's family. The horse becomes ill, and nobody can cure him. A man offers to buy him cheaply, then takes him to Calder Jackson, who "cures" him by the laying on of hands. The Barnets are furious and suspicious.

Indigo (*Bonecrack*). A quiet gelding often ridden as lead horse to the Griffon stable of two-year-olds. Alessandro Rivera rides him often, and his father is displeased. His leg is broken by Alessandro's father.

Irkab Alhawa (*Driving Force*). A sensational horse, trained by Michael Watermead and often driven to races in Freddie Croft's horse vans. "Irkab Alhawa had become almost a cult, the odd-sounding syllables part of his mystique. The press had translated the words into English as 'Ride the Wind,' which had caught the public's imagination . . ."

Jetset ("Blind Chance," *Field of Thirteen*). One of the finishers in a contested race at Ascot.

Kandersteg (*For Kicks*). A horse belonging to sadistic Paul J. Adams. What happens to him provides the final proof Daniel Roke needs to expose the nasty scheme Hedley Humber and Paul J. Adams have been perpetrating.

Laurentide Ice (*The Edge*). Originally owned by Daffodil Quentin. She sells a half share in the racehorse to Julius Apollo Filmer, which allows him to travel in the owners' section of the Great Transcontinental Mystery Racing Train.

Lilyglit ("Haig's Death," *Field of Thirteen*). Owned by Jasper Billington Innes, whose fortunes hang on one big performance.

Lucky Lindsay (*Bonecrack*). A talented but unruly young thoroughbred.

Magic ("Spring Fever," *Field of Thirteen*). A horse of questionable abilities that Mrs. Angela Hart buys, at the suggestion of Clement Scott, as part of her plan to see more of jockey Derek Roberts.

Metavane (*Break In*). Maynard Allardeck bought him from Major and Mrs. Perryside and then syndicated him. The Perrysides, needless to say, did not get a good deal.

Mickey (*For Kicks*). One of the horses belonging to the brutal Paul Adams, whom Daniel Roke suspects plays a key role in the doping scheme he's investigating. The injuries that Daniel discovers on Mickey are a key factor in his solving the puzzle.

Moonrock (*Bonecrack*). Neil Griffon's father's elderly and beloved hack. He "gets cast in his box" one night and breaks his hock.

Moviemaker (*Blood Sport*). One of the missing racehorses Gene Hawkins is seeking.

Neddikins (*Nerve*). The first horse that Rob Finn rides for James Axminster; ". . . a novice hurdler revoltingly called Neddikins, [who] had no chance of winning."

North Face (*Break In*). A bad-tempered horse that Kit Fielding rides to victory in the opening scene, demonstrating his almost psychic connection to the horse he's riding.

Okinawa (*Flying Finish*). A colt who is traveling by air from New York to race in the Derby. He provides Henry Grey with his "first introduction to a horse going berserk in mid-air." Unless Henry can take quick, drastic action, they will have on their hands "a maddened animal loose in a pressurized aircraft with certain death to us all if he got a hoof through a window."

Old Etonian (*For Kicks*). A horse who had gone berserk and killed a woman and was subsequently destroyed. His behavior did not conform to the pattern of the supposedly doped horses Daniel Roke is investigating, but Daniel can't overlook any possible link to the scheme, however obscure it might seem at first.

Ordinand (*The Danger*). A Derby winner who is owned by John Nerrity. Nerrity's son is kidnapped, and the kidnappers tell him to sell the horse for five million to pay their ransom.

Padellic (*High Stakes*). A racehorse owned by Jody Leeds. Padellic looks remarkably like Steven Scott's potential champion, Energise.

Palindrome (*Dead Cert*). Alan York's best horse; the one he is riding at the Cheltenham National Hunt Festival and at Brighton, where he has a nasty accident.

Peterman (*Driving Force*). A former champion, often ridden by Freddie Croft. He is now very elderly and arrives in Freddie's yard with a shipment of old horses being cared for by the dubious charity, Centaur Care.

Pickup ("Blind Chance," *Field of Thirteen*). One of the finishers in a contested race at Ascot.

Pincer Movement ("The Gift," *Field of Thirteen*). Kentucky Derby hopeful, under the training of Harbourn Cressie.

Ramekin (*Proof*). A horse bought by Larry Trent, who subsequently disappears mysteriously.

Revelation (*Odds Against*). A retired Gold Cup winner that Sid Halley rides at Seabury racecourse in order to look for hazards that might sabotage the racing there. He is aptly named, since this ride brings key revelations in Sid's investigation.

River God (*Knockdown*). The second horse that Jonah Dereham buys— and keeps—for Mrs. Kerry Sanders.

Rotaboy (*Banker*). A stallion owned by Oliver Knowles. Rotaboy is getting old, and Oliver wants to replace him at stud with the young and vigorous Sandcastle.

Rudyard (*For Kicks*). One of the horses suspected of having been doped in the ongoing scheme.

Salad Bowl ("The Gift," *Field of Thirteen*). One of the hopefuls in the Kentucky Derby.

Sandcastle (*Banker*). A famous champion racehorse who is purchased for his potential in breeding fast colts. Tim Ekaterin's bank provides the loan for the purchase, and Tim keeps an eye on their investment.

Sarah's Future (*10 Lb. Penalty*). The horse George Juliard buys as a birthday present for his son, Ben. The gift marks a particularly poignant moment between father and son, a symbol of their newfound closeness, since Sarah was the name of Ben's mother, who died after giving birth to him.

Showman (*Blood Sport*). One of the missing racehorses Gene Hawkins is seeking.

Silverboy (*Come to Grief*). A pony owned and much loved by Rachel Ferns, a little girl who is critically ill with leukemia. His hoof is brutally cut off one dark night, and Rachel's mother calls in Sid Halley to investigate.

Six-Ply (*For Kicks*). A horse who may hold part of the key to the truth in the doping scheme Daniel Roke is investigating.

Sparking Plug (*For Kicks*). Horse who is a novice steeplechaser; one of Daniel Roke's first assignments as a stable lad is caring for him.

Sparrowgrass (*The Edge*). A horse, owned by Mr. and Mrs. Young, that is traveling on the race train.

Squelch (*Enquiry*). Kelly Hughes rides Squelch into second place in the Lemonfizz Crystal Cup race at Oxford. A board of enquiry judges that Hughes lost the race deliberately, and warns him off Newmarket Heath.

Starlamp (*For Kicks*). A horse belonging to sadistic Paul J. Adams.

Storm Cone ("Haig's Death," *Field of Thirteen*). Horse that is Lilyglit's chief competition in the race at Winchester Spring Meeting; ridden by Moggie Reilly.

Superman (*For Kicks*). One of the horses Daniel Roke has been investigating. When he runs wild at a race meeting, his appearance and behavior provide information that helps Daniel eventually get to the bottom of a very nasty scheme to fix races.

Tables Turned (*Smokescreen*). One of the South African horses belonging to Nerissa Cavesey. Like her others, it is not performing up to expectations, and no reason can be found for its lack of speed. "We all watched Tables Turned set off at a great rate, run out of puff two furlongs from home, and finish a spent force."

Template (*Nerve*). After Pip Pankhurst is injured, Rob Finn gets his ride on Template and wins. Thereafter, James Axminster gives Rob a job as Pip's replacement. Template and Rob later win a major prize race together, the Midwinter Cup at Ascot, on the day after Rob has been tortured by being hung from a harness hook and left to freeze to death.

Tennessee (*Shattered*). The horse, owned by Lloyd Baxter, that Martin Stukely is riding at Cheltenham when he falls to his death.

Tiddely Pom (*Forfeit*). A horse that is one of the subjects of the plot to rig race results by false forfeits.

Touchy (*Longshot*). A retired Cheltenham Gold Cup winner. Tremayne Vickers asks if John Kendall would like to ride him. It's the first time

Kendall has been on a horse in two years, but he loves the experience of riding Touchy on the gallops so much that he quickly becomes addicted to racing.

Traffic (*Bonecrack*). The Griffon stables' problem colt.

Tri-Nitro (*Whip Hand*). Trained in George Caspar's stable, he is heavily favored to win the Guineas, but loses unexpectedly. His loss may mean the end of the financially troubled stables.

Turniptop (*Nerve*). Owned by James Axminster, Turniptop is the oddly named horse on which Rob proves that, contrary to all rumors, he has not lost his nerve.

Upper Gumtree (*The Edge*). A racehorse traveling on the race train. The horse is owned by the Unwins from Australia. Upper Gumtree wins the big race at Winnipeg, and his owners are thrilled.

Voting Right (*The Edge*). A racehorse on the race train; it is owned by Mercer Lorrimore and is due to race at Vancouver.

Wrecker (*High Stakes*). A racehorse owned by Steven Scott.

Young Higgins (*Hot Money*). Ian Pembroke rides him to victory, much to the owners' (and his father's) satisfaction.

Zingaloo (*Whip Hand*). One of a trio of horses from George Caspar's stable, all of whom were heavily favored to win major races, and unexpectedly failed to do so.

"BOOKS WRITE AUTHORS AS MUCH AS AUTHORS WRITE BOOKS": FIRST LINES AND OTHER QUOTES

Dick Francis often writes riveting opening lines in his novels. Here are a few of the most notable ones:

"I was never particularly keen on my job before the day I got shot and nearly lost it, along with my life." *Odds Against*

"'You're a spoiled, bad-tempered bastard,' my sister said, and jolted me into a course I nearly died of." *Flying Finish*

"I picked four of them up at White Waltham in the new Cherokee Six 300 that never got a chance to grow old. The pale-blue upholstery still had a new leather smell and there wasn't a scratch on the glossy white fuselage. A nice little aeroplane, while it lasted." *Rat Race*

"They both wore thin rubber masks.
    Identical." *Bonecrack*

"I looked at my friend and saw a man who had robbed me."

High Stakes

"I stood on the outside of disaster, looking in."   *In the Frame*

"Thursday, March 17, I spent the morning in anxiety, the afternoon in ecstasy, and the evening unconscious."   *Risk*

"Gordon Michaels stood in the fountain with all his clothes on."   *Banker*

"Kidnapping is a fact of life."   *The Danger*

"Agony is socially unacceptable."   *Proof*

"Blood ties can mean trouble, chains and fatal obligation. The tie of twins, inescapably strongest. My twin, my bond."

Break In

"I intensely disliked my father's fifth wife, but not to the point of murder."   *Hot Money*

"I inherited my brother's life. Inherited his desk, his business, his gadgets, his enemies, his horses and his mistress. I inherited my brother's life, and it nearly killed me."   *Straight*

"I don't think my stepfather much minded dying. That he almost took me with him wasn't really his fault."   *To the Hilt*

"Glue-sniffing jockeys don't win the Derby."   *10 Lb. Penalty*

Then there's the splendid first paragraph of the first book, the one that started it all:

The mingled smells of hot horse and cold river mist filled my nostrils. I could hear only the swish and thud of galloping hooves and the occasional sharp click of horse-shoes striking against each other. Behind me, strung out, rode a group of men dressed like myself in white silk breeches and harlequin jerseys, and in front, his body vividly red and green against the pale curtain of fog, one solitary rider steadied his horse to jump the birch fence stretching blackly across his path.   *Dead Cert*

And this brilliant prologue to *Whip Hand*, set after Sid Halley's mutilated hand has been amputated:

I dreamed I was riding in a race.

    Nothing odd in that. I'd ridden in thousands.

    There were fences to jump. There were horses, and jockeys in a rainbow of colors, and miles of green grass. There were massed banks of people, with pink oval faces, undistinguishable pink blobs from where I crouched in the stirrups, galloping past, straining with speed . . .

    Winning was all. Winning was my function. What I was there for. What I wanted. What I was born for.

    In the dream, I won the race. The shouting turned to cheering, and the cheering lifted me up on its wings, like a wave. But the winning was all; not the cheering.

I woke in the dark, as I often did, at four in the morning.

    There was silence. No cheering. Just silence . . .

There came, at that point, the second awakening. The real one. The moment in which I first moved, and opened my eyes, and remembered that I wouldn't ride any more races, ever . . .

The dream was a dream for whole men.

One discarded dreams, and got dressed, and made what one could of the day.   Whip Hand

Some of our other favorite quotes are:

The jockeys were thrown up like rainbow thistledown onto the tiny saddles and let their skinny bodies move to the fluid rhythm of the walking thoroughbreds. Out on the track with the horses' gait breaking into a trot or canter they would be more comfortable standing up in the stirrups to let the bumpier rhythms flow beneath them, but on the way out from the parade ring they swayed languorously like a camel train. I loved to watch them: never grew tired of it. I loved the big beautiful animals with their tiny brains and their overwhelming instincts . . .   The Edge

Lightheartedness was a treasure in a world too full of sorrows, a treasure little regarded and widely forfeited to aggression, greed and horrendous tribal rituals.   The Edge

The newest foal . . . was born only about twenty minutes ago . . . a glistening little creature half lying, half sitting on the thick straw, all long nose, huge eyes and folded legs, new life already making an effort to balance and stand up. The dam, on her feet, alternately bent her head to the foal and looked up at us warily.   Banker

The law doesn't always deliver justice. The victim mostly loses. Too often the law can only punish, it can't put things right.   Bolt

Give me a horse and a race to ride it in, and I don't care if I wear silks or . . . or . . . pajamas. I don't care if there's anyone watching or not. I don't care if I don't earn much money, or if I break my bones, or if I have to starve to keep my weight down. All I care about is racing . . . racing . . . and winning, if I can.   Nerve

[After a fall]: Oh well, I thought dimly, scraping myself up; six rides, one winner, one second, one fourth, two also-rans, one fall. You can't win four every day, old son. And nothing broken. Even the stitches had survived without leaking. I waited in the blowing sleet for the car to pick me up, and took off my helmet to let the water run through my hair, embracing in a way the wild day, feeling at home. Winter and horses, the old song in the blood.   Kit Fielding in Break In

And finally, Greville Franklin's creed in *Straight* is one that many Dick Francis heroes follow:

May I deal with honour.
May I act with courage.
May I achieve humility.

BIBLIOGRAPHY

WORKS BY DICK FRANCIS
Novels

Dead Cert. London: Michael Joseph, 1962; New York: Holt, 1962.

Nerve. London: Michael Joseph, 1964; New York: Harper, 1964.

For Kicks. London: Michael Joseph, 1965; New York: Harper, 1965.

Odds Against. London: Michael Joseph, 1965; New York: Harper, 1965.

Flying Finish. London: Michael Joseph, 1966; New York: Harper, 1967.

Blood Sport. London: Michael Joseph, 1967; New York: Harper & Row, 1967.

Forfeit. London: Michael Joseph, 1969; New York: Harper, 1969.

Enquiry. London: Michael Joseph, 1969; New York: Harper, 1970.

Rat Race. London: Michael Joseph, 1970; New York: Harper, 1971.

Bonecrack. London: Michael Joseph, 1971; New York: Harper, 1972.

Smokescreen. London: Michael Joseph, 1972; New York: Harper, 1973.

Slay-Ride. London: Michael Joseph, 1973; New York: Harper, 1973.

Knock Down. London: Michael Joseph, 1974. U.S. edition published as *Knock-down*. New York: Harper, 1975.

High Stakes. London: Michael Joseph, 1975; New York: Harper, 1976.

In the Frame. London: Michael Joseph, 1976; New York: Harper, 1977.

Risk. London: Michael Joseph, 1977; New York: Harper, 1978.

Trial Run. London: Michael Joseph, 1978; New York: Harper, 1979.

Whip Hand. London: Michael Joseph, 1979; New York: Harper, 1980.

Reflex. London: Michael Joseph, 1980; New York: Putnam, 1981.

Twice Shy. London: Michael Joseph, 1981; New York: Putnam, 1982.

Banker. London: Michael Joseph, 1982; New York: Putnam, 1983.

The Danger. London: Michael Joseph, 1983; New York: Putnam, 1984.

Proof. London: Michael Joseph, 1984; New York: Putnam, 1985.

Break In. London: Michael Joseph, 1985; New York: Putnam, 1986.

Bolt. London: Michael Joseph, 1986; New York: Putnam, 1987.

Hot Money. London: Michael Joseph, 1987; New York: Putnam, 1988.

The Edge. London: Michael Joseph, 1988; New York: Putnam, 1988.

Straight. London: Michael Joseph, 1989; New York: Putnam, 1989.

Longshot. London: Michael Joseph, 1990; New York: Putnam, 1990.

Comeback. London: Michael Joseph, 1991; New York: Putnam, 1991.

Driving Force. London: Michael Joseph, 1992; New York: Putnam, 1992.

Decider. London: Michael Joseph, 1993; New York: Putnam, 1993.

Wild Horses. London: Michael Joseph, 1994; New York: Putnam, 1994.

Come to Grief. London: Michael Joseph, 1995; New York: Putnam, 1995.

To the Hilt. London: Michael Joseph, 1996; New York: Putnam, 1996.

10 Lb. Penalty. London: Michael Joseph, 1997; New York: Putnam, 1997.

Second Wind. London: Michael Joseph, 1999; New York: Putnam, 1999.

Shattered. London: Michael Joseph, 2000; New York: Putnam, 2000.

Short Stories

Field of Thirteen. London: Michael Joseph, 1998; New York: Putnam, 1998. Includes: "Raid at Kingdom Hill," "Dead on Red," "Song for Mona," "Bright White Star," "Collision Course," "Nightmare," "Carrot for a Chestnut," "The Gift," "Spring Fever," "Blind Chance," "Corkscrew," "The Day of the Losers," and "Haig's Death."

Short Story Anthologies

Francis, Dick, with John Welcome, eds., *Best Racing and Chasing Stories*. London: Faber, 1966.

Francis, Dick, with John Welcome, eds., *Best Racing and Chasing Stories II*. London: Faber, 1969.

Francis, Dick, with John Welcome, eds., *The Dick Francis Treasury of Great Racing Stories*. New York: Norton, 1990.

Francis, Dick, with John Welcome, eds., *The New Treasury of Great Racing Stories*. New York: Norton, 1991.

Francis, Dick, with John Welcome, eds., *The Racing Man's Bedside Book*. London: Faber & Faber, 1969.

Nonfiction

"Can't Anybody Here Write These Games? The Trouble with Sports Fiction." *New York Times Book Review*, June 1, 1986, 56.

A Jockey's Life: The Biography of Lester Piggott. New York: Putnam, 1986. Published in the U.K. as *Lester: The Official Biography*. London: Michael Joseph, 1986.

The Sport of Queens. 1st ed. London: Michael Joseph, 1957; 4th revised ed. London: Michael Joseph, 1999.

Films, Videos Adapted from Dick Francis's Works

Dead Cert (1974). Directed by Tony Richardson. United Artists. Starring Scott Antony and Judi Dench.

The Racing Game. Yorkshire Television, 1979. Includes: "Odds Against"; "Trackdown"; "Gambling Lady"; "Horses for Courses"; "Horsenap"; "Needle." Starring Michael Gwilym and Mick Ford. Shown on *Mystery* (PBS), 1980–81 season. Available on video in two sets of three episodes each from Northstar Entertainment.

Dick Francis Mysteries. Dick Francis Films Ltd., 1989. Includes: *Twice Shy*; *Blood Sport*; *In the Frame*. Starring Ian McShane and Patrick Macnee. Available on video from Northstar Entertainment.

AWARDS

Crime Writers Association Silver Dagger, *For Kicks*, 1965.

Crime Writers Association Gold Dagger, *Whip Hand*, 1980.

Mystery Writers of America Edgar Allan Poe Award for Best Novel:

1969: *Forfeit*

1980: *Whip Hand*

1996: *Come to Grief*

Officer of the Order of the British Empire, 1984.

Commander of the British Empire, 2000.

Honorary doctorate of humane letters degree, Tufts University, 1991.

Grand Master, Mystery Writers of America, 1996.

Elected Fellow of the Royal Society of Literature, 1998.

Lifetime Achievement Award, Malice Domestic Convention, 2000.

WORKS ABOUT DICK FRANCIS
Books

Barnes, Melvyn. *Dick Francis*. New York: Ungar, 1986.

Davis, J. Madison. *Dick Francis*. Twayne, 1989.

Dick Francis: A Reader's Checklist and Reference Guide. Middletown, CT: CheckerBee, 1999.

Fuller, Bryony. *Dick Francis: Steeplechase Jockey.* London: Michael Joseph, 1994.

Goodson, Hesterly Black. *The Voice of the Reader in Dick Francis' Fiction.* Master's degree thesis, University of Vermont, 1987.

Lord, Graham. *Dick Francis: A Racing Life.* London: Little, Brown, 1999.

Articles

Axthelm, Pete. "Writer with a Whip Hand." *Newsweek* 97 (April 6, 1981): 98–100.

Bander, Elaine. "The Least Likely Victim in Dick Francis's *Banker.*" *Clues: A Journal of Detection* 13 (Spring-Summer 1992): 11–19.

Bauska, Barry. "Endure and Prevail: The Novels of Dick Francis." *Armchair Detective* 11 (July 1978): 238–244.

Beyer, Andrew. "Horses Are Essence of Mystery to Francis." *Washington Post,* April 12, 1984, B1.

Bishop, Paul. "The Sport of Sleuths." *The Armchair Detective* 17 (Spring 1984): 144–149.

Callendar, Newgate. "Racing as a Novel Idea." *New York Times,* May 1, 1982, Sec. 1, p. 23.

Cantwell, Robert. "Mystery Makes a Writer." *Sports Illustrated* 28 (March 25, 1968): 76–88.

Carr, John C. "Dick Francis." In *The Craft of Crime: Conversations with Crime Writers.* John C. Carr, ed. Boston: Houghton Mifflin, 1983.

Dampier, Cindy, and Elizabeth Gleick. "As Easy as Falling Off a Horse." *People Weekly* 38 (November 23, 1992): 139–40.

Davis, J. Madison. "Women in Dick Francis." *Clues: A Journal of Detection* 11 (Spring-Summer 1990): 95–105.

DeKoven, Marianne. "Longshot: Crime Fiction as Postmodernism." *Lit: Literature Interpretation Theory* 4 (1993): 185–194.

"Dick Francis." *New Yorker* 45 (March 15, 1969): 29–30.

"Dick Francis." *Current Biography*, 1981, pp. 152–156.

"Dick Francis," In *Contemporary Literary Criticism*. Deborah A. Schmitt, ed., v. 102, pp. 124–164. Detroit: Gale, 1998.

"Dick Francis: An Interview." *The Writer* 103 (July 1990): 9–10.

Fiscella, Joan B. "A Sense of the Under Toad: Play in Mystery Fiction." *Clues* 1 (Fall-Winter 1980): 1–7.

"Francis, Dick." In *Contemporary Authors: New Revision Series*. Daniel Jones and John D. Jorgenson, eds., v. 68, pp. 208–213. Detroit: Gale, 1998.

"Francis, Dick." In *Contemporary Literary Criticism*, Carolyn Riley and Barbara Harte, eds., v. 2, pp. 142–3. Detroit: Gale, 1974.

Francis, Felix. "Was It Dick or Was It Mary? Whodunit?" *Sunday Times*, October 24, 1999.

Gould, Charles E. "The Reigning Phoenix." *Armchair Detective* 17 (Fall 1984): 407–410.

Guttman, Robert J. "Dick Francis: *Europe* Interview." *Europe*, no. 361 (November 1996): 18–21.

Harvey, Deryck. "A Word with Dick Francis." *Armchair Detective* 6 (1973): 151–152.

Helmick, Kristiana. "The Thunder of Racing Hooves Inspires Winning Mysteries." *Christian Science Monitor*, October 27, 1994: 13.

Hochstein, Mort. "Dick Francis, Odds-on Favorite." *Writer's Digest* 66 (August 1986): 32–34.

Keating, H. R. F. "Dick Francis." In *Twentieth Century Crime and Mystery Writers*, John M. Reilly, ed. New York: St. Martin's, 1980.

Keating, H. R. F. "Dick Francis: Overview." In *Contemporary Novelists*, Susan Windisch Brown, ed. 6th ed. St. James Press, 1996.

Killian, Michael. "Champion Rider to Champion Writer." *Chicago Tribune*, November 20, 1990: 1–2.

Klemesrud, Judy. "Behind the Best Sellers: Dick Francis." *New York Times*, June 1, 1980, Sec. 7, p. 42.

Knepper, Marty. "Dick Francis." In *Twelve Englishmen of Mystery*, Earl F. Bargainnier, ed. Bowling Green: Popular Press, 1984.

Lewis, Rae. "Dick Francis Races Between Devon and the Cayman Islands." *Sunday Times*, Oct. 31, 1999.

Macdonald, Gina. "Dick Francis." In *British Mystery and Thriller Writers Since 1940: First Series. Dictionary of Literary Biography*, Bernard Benstock and Thomas F. Staley, eds., v. 87, 136–155. Detroit: Gale, 1989.

Masa, Marja-Liisa. "The World of British Racing (As Seen Through the Novels of Dick Francis)." Unpublished paper for Dept. of Translation Studies, University of Tampere, Finland. URL: http://www.uta.fi/FAST/BIE/BI1/ mlm-race.html#N_28_

McDowell, Edwin. "Teamwork." *New York Times Book Review*, April 12, 1981: 47.

Newcombe, Jack. "Jockey with an Eye for Intrigue." *Life* 66 (June 6, 1969): 81–82.

Sanoff, Alvin P. "Finding Intrigue Wherever He Goes." *U.S. News & World Report*, March 28, 1988.

Schaffer, Rachel. "Dead Funny: The Lighter Side of Dick Francis." *The Armchair Detective* 26 (Spring 1993): 76–81.

Schaffer, Rachel. "The Pain: Trials by Fire in the Novels of Dick Francis." *The Armchair Detective* 27 (Summer 1994): 349–357.

Stanton, Michael N. "Dick Francis: The Worth of Human Love." *Armchair Detective* 15 (1982): 137–143.

Wagner, Elaine. "The Theme of Parental Rejection in the Novels of Dick Francis." *Clues: A Journal of Detection* 18 (Spring-Summer 1997): 7–13.

Wilhelm, Albert E. "Fathers and Sons in Dick Francis's *Proof*." *Critique: Studies in Contemporary Fiction* 32 (Spring 1991): 169–170.

Wilhelm, Albert E. "Finding the True Self: Rites of Passage in Dick Francis's *Flying Finish*." *Clues: A Journal of Detection* 9 (Fall-Winter 1988): 1–8.

Zalewski, James W., and Lawrence B. Rosenfield. "Rules for the Game of Life: The Mysteries of Robert B. Parker and Dick Francis." *Clues* 5 (Fall-Winter 1984): 72–81.

Zuckerman, Edward. "The Winning Form of Dick Francis." *New York Times*, March 25, 1984, Sec. 6, p. 40.

Web Sites
AllReaders.com
http://www.allreaders.com/Topics/Topic_123.asp

Authors and Creators: Dick Francis
http://www.thrillingdetective.com/trivia/francis.html

Buy Books by Dick Francis
http://www.horseworldwide.com/pages/page23.html

ClueLass
http://www.cluelass.com/

Dick Francis
http://members.tripod.co.uk/robin_catchpole/index.html

Dick Francis
http://www.bookbrowse.com/dyn_/author/authorID/342.htm

Dick Francis
http://www.mysteryguide.com/

Dick Francis
http://mysteryinkonline.com/dickfrancis.htm

Dick Francis
http://www.booksnbytes.com/authors/francis_dick.html

Dick Francis
http://wejosephson.home.mindspring.com/dfrancis.htm

Dick Francis
http://www.wellscs.com/ann/reading/dfrancis.htm

Dick Francis

http://members.optushome.com.au/dibingham/francis_main.htm

Dick Francis Books
http://www.pazsaz.com/francis.html

Dick Francis Books.com
http://dickfrancisbooks.com

Dick Francis Discussion
http://pub9.ezboard.com/bdickfrancisdiscussion

Dick Francis *High Stakes* Game
http://www.mobygames.com/game/sheet/gameid=1569/

Dick Francis Interview with Don Swaim
http://wiredforbooks.org/dickfrancis/

Dick Francis, Mystery and Suspense Writer
http://www.hycyber.com/MYST/francis_dick.html

Dick Francis Reading Group
http://members.aol.com/dfbooks/

Dick Francis Reading Group
http://www.readinggroupsonline.com/dfrancis.htm

Dick Francis Trivia at Trivia Wars
http://www.triviawars.com/category/dyn/551

DorothyL
http://www.dorothyl.com

Encyclopedia.com
http://www.encyclopedia.com/html/F/Francisd1i.asp.

Ex Libris Reviews
http://www.wjduquette.com/authors/dfrancis.html

Flying Fish Bookstore
http://www.ffish.com/bookstore/francis.html

If You Like Dick Francis Novels
http://library.christchurch.org.nz/guides/IfYouLike/francis.asp

The Inspirational Dick Francis
http://www.freevote.com/booth/dftalents

iVillagers Interview Dick Francis
http://www.ivillage.com/books/intervu/myst/arti-
    cles/0,11872,240795_97134,00.html

Life and Works of Dick Francis
http://www.dickfrancis.freeservers.com/

Links to Literature
http://www.linkstoliterature.com/francis.htm

MostlyFiction.com
http://mostlyfiction.com/mystery/francis.htm

Mystery Vault
http://www.mysteryvault.net/

100 Masters of Crime
http://www.clarelibrary.ie/eolas/library/services/book-
    promos/100crime/francis.htm

PenguinPutnam catalog
http://www.penguinputnam.com/

Sid Halley
http://www.thrillingdetective.com/halley_sid.html

Stop, You're Killing Me!
http://www.stopyourekillingme.com/Dick-Francis.html

Tales from Francis
http://www.mandry.net/dickfrancis/

Tangled Web
http://www.twbooks.co.uk/authors/dfrancis.html

Unofficial Dick Francis Webpage
http://members.aol.com/kbeale151/dfrancis.html

Yahoo Dick Francis Group
http://groups.yahoo.com/group/dick-francis-group/